## Lift Every Voice Books

Lift every voice and sing
Till earth and heaven ring,
Ring with the harmonies of Liberty;
Let our rejoicing rise
High as the listening skies,
Let it resound loud as the rolling sea.
Sing a song full of the faith that the dark past has taught us,
Sing a song full of the hope that the present has brought us,
Facing the rising sun of our new day begun
Let us march on till victory is won.

The Black National Anthem, written by James Weldon Johnson in 1900, captures the essence of Lift Every Voice Books. Lift Every Voice Books is an imprint of Moody Publishers that celebrates a rich culture and great heritage of faith, based on the foundation of eternal truth—God's Word. We endeavor to restore the fabric of the African-American soul and reclaim the indomitable spirit that kept our forefathers true to God in spite of insurmountable odds.

We are Lift Every Voice Books—Christ-centered books and resources for restoring the African-American soul.

For more information on other books and products
written and produced from a biblical perspective, go to
www.lifteveryvoicebooks.com or write to:

Lift Every Voice Books
820 N. LaSalle Boulevard
Chicago, IL 60610
www.lifteveryvoicebooks.com

Stephanie Perry Moore

Morgan Love Series
Book 1

MOODY PUBLISHERS
CHICAGO

All Scripture quotations are taken from the *New American Standard Bible®*, Copyright © 1960, 1962, 1963, 1968, 1971, 1972, 1973, 1975, 1977, 1995 by the Lockman Foundation. Used by permission. (www.Lockman.org)

Edited by Kathryn Hall
Interior design: Ragont Design
Cover design and image: TS Design Studio
Author photo: Bonnie Rebholz
Word searches by Pam Pugh

Some definitions found at the end of chapters are from WordSmyth.net.

Library of Congress Cataloging-in-Publication Data

Moore, Stephanie Perry.
   A + attitude / Stephanie Perry Moore.
     p. cm. — (Morgan Love series ; #1)
   Summary: Although she is having a hard time adjusting to all the new things in life, especially her new baby brother and stepfather, seven-year-old Morgan makes up her mind that no matter what is going on, she is going to have an A + attitude. Educational exercises provided at the end of each chapter.
   ISBN 978-0-8024-2263-7
   [1. Attitude (Psychology)—Fiction. 2. Remarriage—Fiction. 3. Conduct of life—Fiction. 4. Christian life—Fiction. 5. African Americans—Fiction.] I. Title. II. Title: A plus attitude.
PZ7.M788125Aam 2011
[Fic]—dc22

                              2010048324

Printed by Bethany Press in Bloomington, MN – 09/13


            3 5 7 9 10 8 6 4 2

*Printed in the United States of America*

For
My Paternal Aunt
Virginia Perry Johnson
(Born August 21, 1942)

I am so thankful for a praying aunt like you.
Your charisma is contagious and you're always so positive.
Thank you for letting me know you're proud of my work.
That means more than you know.
I hope every reader gets the message
of this book and acts like you . . .
a lady with pizzazz who loves the Lord and
always displays the sweetest personality!

## Morgan Love Series

# Contents

# Chapter 1

## No Pep

"Morgan Noelle Love! You have got to get out of the car and let go of my waist, girl. I'm going to be late. You're squeezing me like I'm a lemon and you're trying to make lemonade." My dad said this to me as I hugged him tighter than I used to hold my teddy bear, Goldie, when I was in kindergarten. Now that I was going into the second grade, there was a lot going on. Can't a kid get a break?

I am a big girl now. I don't need Goldie to make sure I can sleep at night. I'm big enough to know that the bed bugs won't bite. What I do need is my father, First-Class Captain, Monty Love. He's leaving me again to go back to the U.S. Navy to serve our country off the coast of Africa.

We spent the last two months together, and they were so great. Now our fun time is over. It made me sad to hear him say good-bye, not knowing when he was coming back to Georgia. What will I do without my daddy?

Daddy said, "Morgan, sweetie, I'm serious. I have a plane to catch. It's time for you to go inside your grandparents' house. You see them up there looking out of the window. They can't wait to spend time with you."

I saw them all right. Every time I looked over at their pretty, two-story, red brick house, they jerked away from the window. They didn't want us to think they were spying, but we saw them. And though I loved them very much, I knew that once I went inside their house, I'd lose my dad for a long while—and possibly forever. I could not let him go. I just couldn't.

"I don't want you to leave, Dad. My teacher last year told me that wars are serious fights. This might be the last time I ever see you."

Time. I wanted more of it to share with my daddy, but it was quickly getting away from me. Just like when Papa watches a basketball game and his favorite team is behind and the clock is running out. That makes him real nervous.

Wanting Daddy to understand just how much he means to me, I had to do something real fast. The only thing I could think of at the moment was to shout out. I wanted the whole world to hear me: "I love my country, but why does my dad have to defend it? Couldn't they find someone else?"

To my final attempt, Daddy calmly said, "Now, Morgan, we've gone over all of this before. It's my job to serve in the military, but it won't last forever. That reminds me, baby. I want you to know that all of the letters you send me when I'm away really keep me going. It brings a huge smile to my face to know that I'm keeping my baby girl safe and protecting all the other little children of this great country. I'm so proud of the little lady you are growing up to be, and I know it's going to be hard for us to be apart. But, you know what? You have Jesus in your heart, and He's in my heart too. The Holy Spirit that we talked about is with us. So you don't have to worry about Daddy being safe because God is with me."

He reached into the backseat and pulled out an adorable pink basket tied with a bright pink matching bow. When he handed it to me, I said with surprise, "You got me a present?" My eyes lit up as I held it in my hands. "Wow, it's so beautiful!" All of a sudden, my voice sounded much happier than it had before now.

I couldn't wait another minute to see what was inside, so I ripped off the pretty wrapper. There in the basket was a cute pink notebook with glitter sparkles all over it. It was just the right size to fit in the front pocket of my book bag. On the side of the notebook there was a sparkly pink gel pen with a feather cap. Right away I wanted to use it to write on the fancy matching **stationery**.

Dad could see how excited I was, but I could tell by the look on his face that he was waiting to tell me something important. Pointing to the notebook, he said, "Now, Morgan, this is not a diary. It's your *word keep* book."

"My what?" I asked.

"Your *word keep* book. My baby girl is so smart. And

that's because you love learning new, big words. I want you to keep a log of those words. Write them down along with their meanings. Then use them in your own sentences when you write me letters on your new stationery. That way I'll know what you're learning."

"But I don't want to write letters to you, Daddy. I want you here with me when I learn the new words," I said, as I put the basket down beside me and looked out the window. I didn't want him to see my tears falling. "I want you here to protect me."

"Everything will be okay, Morgan. You have your grandparents here, a mom who loves you more than the world itself, and another daddy that . . . "

He kept talking, but I stopped listening. It's been two years since my parents sat me down and told me that they weren't going to be married anymore. Mommy has a new husband now. To make everything worse, I couldn't go home because she was in the hospital about to have a new baby.

I love my grandparents, Mama and Papa, so much. They made me feel special because I was their only grandchild to love. Soon they were going to have a new grandchild. I was my mom's baby, and now she was having a new baby. I wasn't going to be special Morgan Noelle Love anymore. Was it wrong to be upset?

My dad got out of the car and took my bags out of the trunk. He walked way ahead of me to my grandparents' door. At any other time I would be running ahead of him to get inside and play tea party with Mama or hide-and-seek with Papa. But this day I had no pep in my step.

When they reached down to hug me, I just walked past both of them and went straight upstairs. I had my own bedroom at their house, but that didn't matter. My face was sadder than a girl who didn't get anything for Christmas.

They didn't even bother me. They both knew my heart was broken, and my dad couldn't help me feel better because he had a plane to catch.

When I looked out of the window, I saw Daddy standing by the porch, waving and blowing kisses up at me. I tried so hard to hold back more tears, but I lost the battle. Yes, I was mad at him for leaving me, but I couldn't let him leave without telling him one more time how I felt. So I ran downstairs as fast as I could, jumping over the bottom two stairs.

Everyone knew I would come back for a better goodbye. As I dashed to the door, Mama gave me a basket of goodies to hand to him. My Papa held the door open wide and there stood my dad with his arms stretched out. I jumped into them like I was bouncing on a trampoline.

He picked me up high in the air and spun me around. "You're my little lady, Morgan. Know that you are the most special girl in the world," he said to me.

Daddy kissed me on the forehead and took the basket. Before I knew it, he was gone. My heart felt sad. I already couldn't wait to see him again. But for now, I'd write to him as soon as I could.

• • • • •

"Morgan, let's go, honey," Mama called out to me the next morning.

This was the first day of the second grade, and I was supposed to be super excited. But I couldn't find a way to be happy. Yeah, I had the cutest first-day outfit. I put on my new white shirt with its little pink stars and matching hot pink skirt. The pink and white sneakers Daddy bought me made my outfit look perfect. If no one knew before today that pink was my favorite color, they would know now. My new book bag was loaded with school supplies and I already knew Mama packed some yummy snacks in my lunch box. I couldn't wait to eat the goodies inside.

I really tried to be excited, but there was another thing that made me sad. I wasn't going to know many people at the new school. I was still living in DeKalb County, Georgia, close to the city of Atlanta. But we moved across town after my mom got remarried. Now we live in a new house near her new husband's church. He is a minister at Double Springs Baptist Church.

My life was so messed up because of all the changes going on in everybody else's life. Why did I have to change everything too? Now I had to go to school away from my friends. And that wasn't right.

"Can you pick up the pace a little, Morgan? You're walking slower than a snail," Papa called out as we walked toward the car. "You know I have to get to my train."

Papa was a train conductor, and Mama worked for the mayor of Atlanta. I knew I was moving really slow, but I was so sad. I don't think they knew what I was feeling. Some first day of school! All the other kids had their parents take them to school. Why do my grandparents have to take me and not my own mommy?

"Morgan, do you like Papa's new car?" Mama asked me, as we were about to get inside.

I really wasn't paying it any attention. As far as I knew, it was probably like any other **vehicle**. But after I looked out from the corner of my eye, I had to admit the shiny red convertible was cool. I was just too upset and couldn't force a smile.

The world had done me wrong. My dad was halfway around the world. My mom was in the hospital about to bring home a new baby that I didn't want. I was going to a new school with kids I didn't know. I wasn't supposed to be happy. Not even riding in a new car and feeling my hair blowing in the summer wind was going to make me feel better. No matter what they did or said, no smile was going to be on my face.

As I climbed into the backseat, Papa held the door for me. When he said, "Ooh, Morgan, you're looking good, girl," I knew he was trying to cheer me up. So he went on talking. "That skirt and those little pants underneath work for you. You got it going on, girl!"

"Tommy!" said Mama. "Those are leggings."

"Legging. Pants. Stockings. They're all the same to me," he said.

"Leggings," she corrected him. "It's like I tell you one

day and you forget the next. Now, how many times do I have to tell you?" Mama scolded him, as she playfully nudged him in the arm.

They had the funniest way of fussing at each other. It wasn't like when I lived with my mom and dad. Even when I was small, their fussing made me see that it was hard for them to get along. But Mama and Papa's disagreements were funny. They seemed to have fun picking on each other. It was pretty great.

But still I wasn't going to let them make me laugh. I was too smart and knew that they were talking crazy just to get a smile out of me. It just wasn't going to work. Nope. Today was my mad day, and that was not going to change for anything.

When we pulled up to the school, all of the other kids ran to the car with their *oohs* and *aahs*. My Papa's chest stuck out about a foot long—twelve whole inches. Well, it didn't really stick out that far, but it sure looked like it. He acted really proud and stuff. He was showing the boys how to let the top down. The girls were checking out my Mama. They couldn't help but notice the huge smile on her face because she was so proud of Papa.

After Mama and I got out of the car one of the girls from the crowd came over to me and said, "Your grandparents are the coolest." Then she raised her hand like I was going to give her a high-five or something.

Didn't she know that this was my mad day? I rolled my eyes at her and crossed my arms. I wasn't going to speak to her or anyone else. This was not the day to mess with me, and I meant it.

"Hi, I'm Brooke," the girl said, not caring that I wasn't acting friendly.

"This is Morgan," Mama said, as if I couldn't speak for myself.

I looked back over my shoulder and gave her a look as if to say, *I don't want you to be here. I don't want you to speak for me, and I don't want to make any new friends.* My grandmother just hung her head low like she gave up. She was always a **sassy** lady, and my dad said I got my personality from her. I couldn't remember ever seeing her sad and not knowing what to say. Mama didn't even respond and just walked away, **dejected**.

Brooke said, "That was mean. I couldn't talk to my mom that way."

"I didn't *say* anything to her," I said, setting the record straight.

"Well, if I even looked at my mom that way . . . " Brooke said before I huffed and walked away from her.

• • • • •

Inside the classroom, this crazy and out-of-control boy was running and almost knocked me down.

"Hey, watch where you're going!" I said to him, thinking, *Boys! Ugh! They're so rough!*

He made me so mad that I had to look down at my clothes to make sure everything was okay. Then I said,

17

"You'd better not get me dirty. Stu—"

Before I could get out the rest of the word "stupid," Papa called out, "Morgan Noelle Love! What has gotten into you?"

**Frustrated**, I turned to him and Mama. "Why are you both still here? Everyone else's parents have left."

"Because we love you, honey, and we want to make sure you settle in okay," Mama replied.

"I'm okay. There's Miss Nelson sitting at her desk, so you can leave."

Papa asked, "How did you know her name was Miss Nelson?"

"All summer long, I knew whose class I'd be in, Papa. Ugh," I said and stormed to my seat. It was a mean thing to say, and I should've just told him that Mommy gave me my new teacher's name on the day she enrolled me in school.

A classmate tried to make up for me by telling my grandpa, "Don't worry about her, mister. She's just a girl, and sometimes they're plain weird." Later I learned his name was Trey.

But my granddad had a sad face, and I turned away so I wouldn't see him. Finally, Mama and Papa left. I should have felt bad that I had such a stinky attitude. But with them gone, for the moment I felt a little better.

"Miss Love, I want to see you for a second," Miss Nelson called to me. She was pretty and tall, with a calm voice. Her smile made me feel like I was looking at an angel, but I still knew I was in trouble. I hadn't been in her classroom for ten minutes before she needed to see me. No good was coming out of this.

"Yes, ma'am?"

"I just want you to know that you were very mean to your grandparents. I've watched you since you came into the room, and you've been mean to your classmates too. I don't know what's going on with you, young lady, but you'd better fix it quickly. In my classroom, we all get along. If you don't want to do that, then we can take a nice trip to the principal's office."

Miss Nelson wasn't playing around. She was spelling out exactly what she wanted me to know, as she continued, "So I suggest you zip that lip and take in what I'm saying to you. Now, we can either have a nice year or it can be a long and hard one—if you get on my bad side. Go back to your seat and figure out which way you want it to be."

Gritting my teeth, I screamed on the inside. Miss Nelson didn't know what I was going through and now she was going to force me to be nice. What was I going to do? So far, second grade was yucky.

•  •  •  •  •

Finally, it was almost the end of the first day of school. I kept catching Brooke looking over at me. Though I wasn't rolling my eyes anymore, I wasn't smiling either. I didn't want to be her friend. I missed Kimberly and Jan at my old school. These new kids were going to take some getting used to.

Trey kept trying to make me laugh. He was making silly moves like he couldn't be still and saying raps that didn't **rhyme**. I couldn't understand why he was acting like such a clown.

Then Miss Nelson divided us into groups for the math team game. She made Trey captain of one team, and Brooke was captain of the other. Neither one of them picked me and that didn't feel good. I started thinking it wasn't cool for people not to like me. It kinda hurt to overhear kids saying, "Don't pick her. She's mean. If she's on our team, we'll lose for sure with her bad attitude."

With twenty-four students in our class, I was the last one sitting in my seat. It was Brooke's turn to pick. She looked at me and then looked away.

"Ha!" Trey said, laughing out loud. "You get Morgan."

Wow. The girl who clearly wanted to be my friend earlier didn't even want me to be on her team now.

*I'll show them,* I thought to myself.

The game was going to be a fun math review. Miss Nelson wrote an addition or subtraction problem on the board and the first team who got the answer right scored the point. I don't know what everybody else was doing for the summer, but I was on the money. Everywhere my dad and I went—like Six Flags or the World of Coca-Cola—we counted things like people, rides, animals, and even our steps.

The problem on the board was "Five elephants, plus six giraffes, plus three monkeys, is how many animals?"

Because of all the practice I'd had, I knew the answer was fourteen animals. I didn't have to count on my fingers like Trey was doing. And I didn't need to count the numbers aloud like Brooke.

"This is mental math. I know the answer," I told them.

Truly wanting to win, Brooke said, "Then tell us the answer."

"Why should I help you when you didn't even want me on your team? I should let the team lose just because you wouldn't pick me."

"Aw, she doesn't know the answer," said Kyle, another boy on our team.

"I sure do," I replied and sat back down in my chair to watch Trey's team clobber ours.

For mental math, there are some simple rules. Ten plus any single digit number adds a one in front of that number. For example, $10 + 6 = 16$. If you have a nine and add a single digit number to it, the sum is a one and one less than the single digit number. For example, $9 + 7 = 16$. Most equations you just need to practice and memorize. Then once you know it, it is mental math. For example, $8 + 7 = 15$.

Subtraction is easy as well. I used flash cards to practice learning them. Plus my dad and I practiced subtraction all summer with money. He'd give me a twenty dollar bill, and every time I asked for something that day money was taken from the twenty dollars. For example, if I wanted a soda that was $2 and a burger that was $4, I added those together, which is $6. Then my new equation was $20 - $6 = $14. And that's what I had left over.

Most people in the class said they didn't study math over the summer and I could tell. It took both teams a while to get all the easy answers. Still, when the game was over, we'd lost big time. Miss Nelson assigned the losing team math worksheets for homework. Brooke and all the kids on our team were upset with me. But it wasn't going to bother me that we had to do math homework. I looked at that easy sheet and knew I could finish it in about five minutes.

When Miss Nelson said it was time for recess, everyone got up and cheered. I sat still. I guess it made me weird to like classwork. I liked learning more than having free time to run around and act crazy. But then Miss Nelson made me go out and have fun with the other kids. Everyone was running, smiling, and jumping. I did look kinda silly sitting on a bench with my arms folded.

So I whispered a prayer. "God, help me. I don't want to be so angry. It just doesn't seem fair. Everything that I didn't want to happen to me is happening even though I was good. My parents told me it wasn't my fault they weren't together anymore, but it hurt so bad to not have them together.

Besides, I've lived for this long without a baby brother or sister, why do I have to have one now? You're supposed to take care of me and love me. It doesn't seem fair. Can You put a smile on my face?"

"Who are you over here talking to?" Brooke asked, as she came and sat next to me.

I quickly turned away from her. "I'm talking to God. Is that a crime?"

"Okay, okay. Why do you have to be so mean? Do you think He'll be happy with the way you're acting?"

That was a good question. When my dad took me to Sunday school last week, we talked about Job. He was a man who had money, a big family, and happiness. But when Job lost everything he had, he didn't get angry about it. This is what he said about it in Job 1:21, "The Lord gave and the Lord has taken away. Blessed be the name of the Lord." It was one thing to read that, but was I supposed to live it?

Brooke kept talking to me. "I know you're new here, and you're probably upset that you can't see your old friends too. But how do you think we feel? I'm mad that my parents couldn't buy me a new outfit for my first day, and I really like how cool you're dressed. But I'm not going to get mad at you because you have something I want. So don't you be mad at me. Okay?"

"I'm not mad at you, Brooke."

"Then quit acting like it. Nobody picked you today because you've been mean all morning. I don't care what anybody says, everyone wants to have friends. Think about it."

Then she got up to play with the other girls around us. I couldn't wait for the day to end. I didn't know how to tell

Brooke I wanted to be her buddy too. Even though I was going through some **horrible** things, I just didn't know how to fix my bad attitude. So I was left there by myself to sulk and be sad. My mouth was closed and I had no pep.

## Letter to Dad

Dear Dad,

You see I'm using the **stationery** you got me to write you a letter. I miss you so much. My first day of school was not cool. Though Papa drove me there in his pretty new **vehicle** you'd love, I was a bit **sassy**. I'm just unhappy you're gone, and I don't want a baby brother. The first day was bad because no one picked me for the math team and I felt **dejected**. To be honest, I'm very **frustrated** that I'm not at my old school with my old friends. It's not cool to be at this school. That is a **rhyme**. Right now I feel **horrible** that I have to go back tomorrow.

Your daughter,
Mad, Morgan

# Word Search

```
M O R G A N L U V D S C
J S T A T I O N E R Y A
A E C O M E Q T D H D N
Y K M O K Q A U N Y U D
D O M R E R L O I M Q E
E D L D T R Y Y K E P T
N R W S A S S Y E T U C
T B U C S C H O O L O E
O R X B E L C I H E V J
F T R E Y Z G D P X N E
S L R I G T H G I R B D
A T L A N T A R O C K S
```

**DEJECTED**

**FRUSTRATE**

**RHYME**

**SASSY**

**STATIONERY**

**VEHICLE**

# Words to Know and Learn

1) **stationery** (stā'shə-nĕr'ē) *noun*
Writing paper and envelopes

2) **ve·hi·cle** (vē'ĭ-kəl) *noun*
Something used to carry persons or things

3) **sas·sy** (săs'ē) *adjective*
Rude and disrespectful

4) **de·ject·ed** (dĭ-jĕk'tĭd) *adjective*
In low spirits; sad

5) **frus·trate** (frŭs'trāt') *transitive verb*
Feeling discouraged or baffled

6) **rhyme** (rīm) *noun*
A word that ends with the same sound as another word

7) **hor·ri·ble** (hôr'ə-bəl, hŏr'-) *adjective*
Very unpleasant; disagreeable; very bad

# Chapter 2

# Real Sad

Riding home on a noisy yellow school bus wasn't something I was used to doing. **Torture** was what it was. There were kids singing at the top of their lungs to whatever came to their mind, while others chatted about how awesome their first day was or how great their teacher was. They even talked about the new friends they made. I just sat alone on the deep, dark, black bus seat.

If my mom wasn't in the hospital right now having her baby, she would have been there to pick me up like she did when I was in kindergarten and the first grade. Mom promised me that nothing would change when she had the baby, but my life was already different. Boy, I really don't like that.

The sun was shining bright. It was 92 **degrees** in Georgia in the middle of August, but in my heart it seemed like the middle of winter. My sad heart felt like gray clouds forming on a stormy day. Why couldn't I be happy?

Then, when I started thinking about the food Mama would have waiting for me, I felt better. Sitting there on that bumpy bus, I started rubbing my tummy. The highlight of my day had been eating a grilled chicken sandwich and a wonderful slice of her strawberry cake at lunchtime. Just thinking about having another piece of that cake made me feel not so down.

When the bus pulled up in front of my grandparents' house, I saw the red convertible in the driveway. What was Papa doing home? He was supposed to be on the train heading to Tennessee. I thought we weren't supposed to see him again for a few days. When I went into the house and ran to the kitchen, Mama didn't have milk and cake waiting for me. Instead, I heard voices from the family room and something that sounded like crying.

"She's got to be okay, Tommy."

"Who's got to be okay?" I asked, knowing I was never supposed to listen in on a grown-up conversation.

When my grandmother saw me standing there, she came rushing to me and hugged me real tight. "Oh, Morgan!"

Papa said, "Stop with all that crying. You're going to scare the child."

Papa was right. I was shaking. What was going on? Mama wiped her tears and tried to speak but no words came. I was waiting for her to tickle me or for Papa to crack a joke but they didn't do either. This had to be something big.

"We have to go to the hospital, Morgan," Mama finally said, letting me in on the **dilemma**.

"The hospital? What's wrong? Did Mom have the baby yet? It seems like it's taking a long time."

Mama took my hand and said, "There have been some **complications**, honey."

"What does that mean?" I asked. I could tell by the way Mama said the word that it wasn't a word I wanted to understand. I knew it related to my mommy and her being in the hospital. "Complications" didn't sound like a good word, and that made my stomach drop worse than when Daddy and me were on a roller coaster a few weeks back.

"Oh, don't worry. Everything's gonna be okay. I promise," Papa said, acting as if Mama's reaction wasn't a big deal.

*Come on people! I'm growing up. I'm a big girl now.* I could see Mama was sad, and I knew something serious was going on. I wanted to know. So I said to them, "If everything is okay, then why aren't you at work, Papa? I know Mama took off early to be here when I came from school, but you're supposed to be in Tennessee. What's happening? Is something wrong with Mommy?"

Papa didn't answer me, and I was getting more worried. Mama tried to force a smile but it wasn't **soothing** to me. This was crazy! She knew I was hungry since I had just come from school, so she grabbed an apple and a bottle of water for our trip to the hospital.

My face wasn't happy at all. "These complications aren't good, huh?" I asked, still getting no answer.

I could've kicked myself. I had spent the last couple months away from my mom because I was with my dad.

And I was happy that I could be with him before he left for the Navy. But I wasn't happy about the fact that Mom had a new husband.

She and my stepdad, Mr. Derek, were excited about the new baby. I didn't see where I belonged in that picture. And as much as she told me that she loved me, a part of me truly was upset with her. Now here we were in the parking lot of a huge, scary building, and I wished I could take back every mean thing I'd said about my mom.

"We need to pray," Mama said.

"Before we do," I spoke up, "I want to apologize for being so mean when you all came to my school." My bad behavior had been on my mind, and I wanted them to forgive me.

"It's okay, sweetheart. We love you, but we do expect for you to act better," Papa said before he began to pray.

"Lord, You already know why we're coming to You right now. Lift up our daughter and Morgan's mom. Please give us the peace we need so we won't worry about anything. We do ask that You make her better. In Jesus' name."

"Amen," said Mama.

I just looked up at heaven with eyes like a puppy dog who wanted to come inside from the rain. I hoped God heard our prayer and would answer. We needed Him.

● ● ● ● ●

When we got to the floor my mother was on, I saw my stepdad, Mr. Derek, sitting with his hands over his face.

"Derek, honey, are you okay?" Mama asked.

"Yes. It's going to be all right. Everything is okay." He looked at me and came over to give me a big hug. "You guys need to see her. They may not let you go in, but you can ask. I'll sit here with Morgan."

Mr. Derek was trying to fight the pain, but I could tell it was hurting him bad inside. I was becoming even more afraid. Mom always told me that I was her best friend. I guess it was because she and I had to rely on each other when everything fell apart between her and Dad. She never talked to me like an adult, but she didn't baby talk me either. Whenever her friends or my grandparents came over and talked about some kind of trouble, I grew to understand when something was wrong.

I didn't know Mr. Derek well, but I knew that my mom loved him and he loved my mom. He was a nice guy to her and was never mean to me. Now Mom had a new best friend—and that hurt. Though I didn't realize I cared for him, seeing him broken up that Mom was in trouble made me want to reach out to him. I wanted to fix our problems.

"It's okay, Mr. Derek. You can tell me what's going on with my mom. She would want you to tell me if something was wrong. I know it. Please tell me."

"I'm sorry, Morgan. I know I'm not your dad, and I'm not trying to take his place. You have an amazing father that loves you. But I look at you like you're my own daughter. You are a big girl, and I know your mom talks to you about tough stuff, but right now we really don't know what's going on with her."

"So, did she have the baby?" I asked.

"Yes, she did. You have a little brother. But they had to operate to save him and now she's very weak. She hasn't woken up yet."

Something inside me made me grab his hand and squeeze it tight. Mr. Derek's head hung low. When he lifted it and looked over at me, I said, "My mommy is strong. She's a fighter, and she will make it through this."

He smiled a little and replied, "Look at you. A sweet girl like you is giving me hope. She is strong, isn't she?"

"She always told me that she's stronger than a Mack truck, but I have no idea what that means."

Mr. Derek sat up, saying, "Okay. Here's my first daddy teaching time. Cool. A Mack truck weighs tons. They are those big heavy trucks that carry a lot of rocks and heavy things. They sometimes use them to move cars across the highways. They're stronger than any car, and I don't think anyone could pick one up."

"So Mommy is stronger than that," I said, and he nodded his head.

"Like I told you, Mr. Derek, Mom is going to be okay."

"Your mom missed you this summer," he told me, as he reached down under his seat and pulled out a big gift basket of my favorite brownies, chocolate-covered pretzels, and a super soft teddy bear.

"Thanks, but what's this for? I'm not a baby."

"It's from your baby brother."

"Is he going to be okay?"

"Well, he's a little small, but he's a trouper. Everything will be fine, including him and your mother. If you want, we can go and see him and all the other little babies."

We picked up our belongings from the seat in the waiting area and walked down the long hallway. When we stopped at a huge glass window, a nurse brought the tiny infant to the window. He was adorable. Now I don't remember being a baby, but I do remember all the pictures my mom and Mama had around. He looked just like me except he was a boy.

Looking at his precious face made me happy again. I couldn't believe I was a big sister! I hugged Mr. Derek tight. Before I didn't think I wanted him as a stepdad. Now things were different. Together we were going to get through this. I had prayed earlier with my grandparents, and I just knew everything was going to be okay. It just had to be.

●　●　●　●　●

"Why does she look so sad?" Brooke said to Trey.

The next day at school my head was down when we first walked into the building.

"Because she's crazy!" Trey yelled. "One day she's mad, and the next day she's sad. Ugh! Girls."

I definitely didn't want to be at school. No one would understand that I wasn't feeling well. I begged Mama and Papa not to send me to school so I could go to the hospital with them. They said that getting an education was more important, and I needed to keep my mind on positive things.

But how could I be happy? All summer long I hadn't spoken to Mom except for the times Daddy made me. Even then the phone **conversations** were short. Now she was in the hospital, and I wanted so much to tell her everything.

Miss Nelson started class by saying, "Last year, you all learned about nouns and verbs. Remember nouns are a person, a place, or a thing. And verbs are words that describe action. Today we are going to learn about **adjectives**. Does anyone know what adjectives are?"

From the silence in the classroom, I could tell no one knew the answer. I looked down at my desk and wondered which student was going to answer her question.

Then she said, "Morgan, do you know what an adjective is?"

*Why did she pick on me?* I thought. Then I answered, "I think it's a word that describes another word, Miss Nelson."

"Okay, great. Well, can you come to the board, write a sentence, and underline the adjective?"

"She can't do all that. She really isn't that smart," Trey yelled out being silly as usual.

"I know she can do it," Brooke said, defending me.

I sort of gave a grin and tried my best to keep my teeth from showing through my lips. Wow! That was really nice of Brooke to say. Even when I hadn't reached out to her, she was still saying really nice things about me. Yesterday when we were in the pencil sharpener line, she told people to be nice to me. She didn't want them to say mean things about me.

I felt bad that she was trying to be my friend when I wasn't trying to be her buddy. Maybe she didn't think I'd noticed, but I did.

Holding a green marker in my hand, I went to the board and tried to come up with a sentence, but I couldn't. Looking around the classroom, I was searching for something to describe. The fish tank? No. The size of the desks? No. Finally, it came to me and I wrote: Miss Nelson has on a red shirt. Then I underlined red.

"Very good, Morgan. Red is an adjective. Adjectives describe the noun and make the sentence more interesting. You're exactly right. It's not just a shirt. It's a red shirt. It could also be described as a 'cotton shirt' or maybe as a 'pretty shirt'."

"But not Trey's shirt," another girl called out from the other side of the room.

"Ha ha ha," Trey called out at her.

"That's enough, class. We're learning. Adjectives used the right way can make having a conversation more fun. What kind of day is it today, Morgan?"

I couldn't even answer her with a good adjective. Today was a gloomy day. It was a dark day, and it was a horrible day. Actually, for me it was the worse day ever! I just dashed out of the room and went into the girls' bathroom. Before I could even get well into my tears, Miss Nelson came in to check on me.

"Morgan, what's wrong? I have a message to call your

grandmother. When I called, I got her voice mail. Are you okay?"

"My mommy is in the hospital."

"I knew she was having a baby. Is she okay?"

"I don't want to be in school. She needs me to be with her." All of a sudden, I was crying more than any of the babies I'd seen at the hospital yesterday.

Miss Nelson handed me a paper towel. "Oh, sweetheart, I don't know your mother, but I know she would want you to be strong. You're a big sister and a big girl."

"I know she would, Miss Nelson, and I'm trying really hard. But if something happens to her—"

"Now, Morgan, let's take it one minute at a time. How many seconds is that?"

Between sobs, I huffed, "Sixty."

"Good. Now, how many minutes are in one hour?"

With tears slowing, I said, "Sixty."

"Now, we'll just take it one second, one minute, and one hour at a time. Then, before you know it, the end of the day will come, and you can go home. Don't worry; it'll be okay before then."

"You think so, Miss Nelson?" Whether she thought so or not, when she smiled at me, I felt so much comfort. It was like my teacher was some kind of angel sent from God above to make me feel better.

Later that day on the playground, Brooke and Trey came over to me. Trey had his hands in his pockets and was kicking at the dirt. Brooke was grinning ear to ear, with a smile the size of the state of Texas.

"So, uh, just so you know, I was the smartest kid in first grade. And now you know all the answers. So even though you're a girl, you're going to have to be my buddy," Trey said so quickly I didn't catch all of his words.

"What?" I asked.

Brooke laughed. "He's trying to say that he doesn't like not being the smartest kid in the class."

"Well, it's like my mom says, 'if you can't beat 'em, join 'em.' That's it," he said and then ran off.

"Look, we didn't mean to come and interrupt your time alone. You look like you need it," Brooke said, pointing at my red eyes.

"No, I'd like it better if you stay," I said to her, trying to smile.

"You want me to stay?" she asked in surprise.

"Yeah. I'm sorry I've been so mean. It's been a lot of crazy things going on. My mom is married again. Now she's in the hospital, and I'm worried about her. I guess with all the stuff I got going on, it hasn't made me the nicest person. But you told me yesterday that I wasn't being a good Christian girl, and that's not right. I want God to smile down on me from heaven and make it better. You're the kind of friend I need. Not to just tell me what I want to hear, but to also tell me what I need to hear."

"It's okay to be worried about your mom," she said in a soft voice. "I'll pray for her, and I'll pray for you. Here's a number you can reach me at. It's my sister's cell phone, but she lets me talk on it sometimes. When you get the good news about your mom, call me. Then you won't be real sad."

## Letter to Dad

Dear Dad,

Today was better at school. I have a new friend. Her name is Brooke. You'd like her. She keeps me honest. She said I was being a **torture** to everyone. I think everyone was trippin' because it's so hot here. It's 90 **degrees**. I was sort of mean, but I do have a **dilemma**.

Mom had the baby with some **complications**. You would like to hear that Mr. Derek said some **soothing** words to calm me down. I think he may be okay after all. I really enjoyed our **conversation**. He said Mom would be okay. Oh yeah, in school my homework is to write three **adjectives** in a sentence. So here is one. My dad is a fun, brave, and super man!

Your daughter,
Scared for Mom, Morgan

## Word Search

```
C O N V E R S A T I O N
S C H O O L O M I S S O
P E R R Y J O L D S N I
E R U T R O T Q E B E T
M O N D A Y H V G F L A
A M O O R E I R R W S C
T M P A T T N A E P O I
Y K M R C X G E E A N L
P E Z E R E A D S M Z P
E M J X L M O R G A N M
S D C A T I R Y E O J O
A E K O R B D E V O L C
```

**ADJECTIVES**

**COMPLICATION**

**CONVERSATION**

**DEGREES**

**DILEMMA**

**SOOTHING**

**TORTURE**

# Words to Know and Learn

**1) tor·ture** (tôr'chər) *noun*
Something causing severe mental or physical pain

**2) de·gree** (dĭ-grē') *noun*
A unit for measuring temperature

**3) di·lem·ma** (dĭ-lĕm'ə) *noun*
A situation that requires a choice between two actions, neither of which may be a good solution

**4) com·pli·ca·tion** (kŏm'plĭ-kā'shən) *noun*
Something that makes a situation, event, or condition more difficult

**5) sooth·ing** (sū'thĭng) *adjective*
Having a calming or relieving effect

**6) ad·jec·tive** (ăj'ĭk-tĭv) *noun*
The part of speech that describes another word

**6) con·ver·sa·tion** (kŏn'vər-sā'shən) *noun*
The spoken exchange of thoughts, opinions, and feeliings; talk

# Chapter 3

## Great News

Everything seemed so right when I opened the door to my grandparents' home after coming from school. I heard music coming from Mama's bedroom. The closer I moved toward the door, I knew it was one of her favorite songs. She was singing along with the music. I could tell that she was in a happy mood because she loved scented candles and only lit them for a good occasion. Walking down the hallway, I counted six candles in all.

My tummy was growling so loud that a lion couldn't beat it. I hadn't eaten anything since lunchtime at school, and now I was ready to "chew a cow," as Mommy would say. But I wouldn't be disappointed if there was no snack in sight, with all that happened yesterday.

Then, to my surprise, when I peeked in the kitchen, I

spotted a large slice of strawberry cake on a plate with a tall glass of milk beside it. I really hoped that it was for me and was happy to read the note laying next to it:

*Morgan,*
*I hope you had a wonderful day. Eat up!*
*Love, Mama*

I wanted to sit down right away and enjoy the delicious cake, but for some reason there were butterflies in my stomach. Maybe they were hungry too because something was definitely telling me to be excited. But why? I had to find out what it was. So I put my book bag down and went to look for Mama. She was still in her bedroom with the door closed. I knocked quietly.

"Come in," she said, dancing around. When I walked in, her face lit up the room. "We need to get you into ballet lessons, girl," Mama said, as she began twirling me around and lifting me into the air.

Now I was excited too! I always wanted to be a ballerina ever since the first time I saw them twirl around on TV. Mommy was planning to sign me up so I could take lessons. Just the thought of me floating on air made me smile. But then I remembered that I had come to find out what was going on.

Yeah, I was growing up. Before I left for school this morning, we hadn't heard any good news about my mom. Mama was a bit cranky; not mean, but just not like this.

Now, she had joy in her eyes and love in her smile. What changed?

I really wanted her to stop twirling me so I tugged away. Mama said, "You don't wanna dance?"

"I'm worried about my mommy. I just can't keep **pretending** everything is okay when it's not. I know you're trying to keep my mind off of **negative** things, fixing my favorite treats and having the house smell so good. But Mommy's in the hospital and everything's not right."

She fell to her knees and hugged me tight. "Oh, Morgan Noelle Love, you have such a big heart. You don't wanna have fun when someone else is in pain. Well, that's great because I'm not trying to keep it a secret. Honey, your mom is fine!"

Shouting every last word at the top of her lungs, it brought me joy. I probably could've heard her if I was at my school. Even if it did hurt my ears, I would've loved for her to scream what she said over and over again.

So I shouted back like I was on the playground. I said, "Really, Mama? My mom is okay? I can't believe it!"

I helped my grandmother off of the floor, and we danced a happy dance. Pushing me toward the kitchen, she said, "Believe it, child. Now hurry up and finish that cake so we can go and see her."

Then that's what I was gonna do. So we both went into the kitchen, and I couldn't wait to say a prayer and eat my delicious cake. I was going to see Mommy, and we were going to be so happy!

Mama watched me while I ate. "Miss Morgan, we're going to have to teach you some manners."

"Mmmmm-mhmmm . . . but its mmmmmmm!" I mumbled as I gulped down the cake and drank my milk.

"I can't understand you, girl. You know you're not supposed to talk with your mouth full."

Finally, when I swallowed the last bite, I said, "I'm just trying to hurry to the hospital. I'm so excited, Mama!"

"I know, baby, and we'll get there. Now, clean up your mess so we can leave."

I put my plate and glass in the dishwasher to prove to her that I was a big girl. Then I had to brush my teeth and wash my face so that I was fresh for Mommy. When I was done, I was ready to go. But then the telephone rang. It was Papa. Mama couldn't get a breath in while she was telling him the good news. I heard him shouting for joy too. We were all so happy. As soon as they hung up, I walked to the door, but Mama stopped me.

"Wait, Morgan. There's something I need to get." She took a vase from under the kitchen sink. "I need to pick some flowers from my garden to take to your mom."

Carefully, she cut the pretty flowers and put them in the vase. Then just as I thought we were on our way, the doorbell rang. I sighed because these **distractions** were getting out of hand!

"Oh, no. It's Miss May. Not right now," Mama said to me, as she looked out the pretty wood-and-glass door.

Miss May was my grandmother's best friend and next

door neighbor. Boy, could she talk your right and left ears off. She talked more than me, my grandmother, and my mother put together. Everybody knew if you were in a rush the last person to speak to was Miss May.

Mama quickly opened the door. "Hey, May. Can't chat too long because as I told you earlier, as soon as Morgan got home from school we were headed to the hospital."

"Oh, Sarah. This ain't gonna take nothin' but a second. Move on out the way so I can tell you this good news. Of course, it ain't as good as your daughter bein' well, but I'm gonna go ahead and tell you! You know that we've all been prayin' for my baby to get a j-o-b. Well, the good Lord has come through. My daughter, Sharon, found a job. She had been going to job after job after job, and I was getting worried . . . thought she was gon' have to move in with me. The way she hogs the TV, I couldn't have that. Now that she's got a job, she won't have to move in," Miss May went on and on.

Mama stepped in front of her. "That's good to hear, May. I'm sure I'll hear more about it later. But we have to go now."

Miss May didn't get the hint. She pushed her way inside anyway. "Give me a second, and I can fill you in with the details."

Mama let her come all the way inside to finish her story. I was becoming more and more upset. For once in a long time, I was really excited to see my mom and now I had to wait longer just to hear about some lady getting a new job. My face was saying, *Mama, can we go?* But her face was saying, *I shouldn't have opened the door.* We both had to wait patiently in the family room for Miss May to stop talking.

And she kept going on, "Can you believe it? Sharon found a job. I can't believe it. It took her forever to realize that the reason she wasn't getting a job was because of her attitude. I told her long before that she needed to work on herself. But I'm proud of her and hope this one works out for her. See, she don't have a degree like your daughter, so her job choices are limited. But she got one now. Sharon got a job."

I looked at the big **mahogany** grandfather clock in the hallway. The hands seemed like they were moving faster than I wanted them to. My mind was on getting to Mommy and that was it. I wasn't listening to what Miss May was saying.

Then she snapped her finger at me. "Morgan, I want you to listen closely now. Don't grow up around here with no bad attitude. You won't get too far or get what you need in this world. You hear me now?"

"Yes, ma'am, Miss May."

She asked, "You got any questions?"

"Can I go see my mommy now?"

"What! Well, why didn't y'all say so? I knew I had good news but I didn't wanna stop y'all from goin' to the hospital. Get on out of here!"

Mama and I walked outside with Miss May and

watched her cross over her yard. We laughed all the way to the hospital, thinking about how we were just trying to keep the peace. All we had to do was remind her that we had to go.

• • • • •

When we got to the hospital, the doctors were running tests on Mom. Mama couldn't wait so she went to see the baby. I wanted them to hurry up because I was ready to see Mommy, talk to her, and hug her.

"Are you Morgan Noelle Love?" a kind, blonde-haired lady asked me while I sat in the waiting room. She had blue eyes, the most blue I've seen outside of a crayon box.

"Yes, I am. May I see my mommy now?"

The nice nurse said, "You sure can, honey. She's been waiting for her big girl all day."

She looked down at the flowers in my hand and said, "Those are really going to make her day."

"Yeah. My grandma and I planted them last summer, and now they're in full bloom. Daisies and roses."

"She's a special lady to get those kinds of flowers."

"Well, here. You take a rose since you've been taking special care of my mom. Thank you so much for making her well. Think of this as me paying part of her hospital bill."

"Why, thank you. You are a big girl. And so sweet at that." She laughed and hugged me.

As she walked me to Mom's room, I didn't know why

she was laughing. I would've given her my whole piggy bank if I had it with me. Since she was part of the team that helped my mom get better, then she was extra special too. I was glad a rose could make her day.

"Morgan," Mom said in a weak voice, but still the best one I'd ever heard.

"Mommy!" I said, running over to hug her tight.

"Oh," she said in pain.

"I'm sorry, Mommy. I didn't mean to hurt you."

"Baby, I'm okay. I want you to hug me. I missed you, Morgan."

"Mommy, I'm so sorry," I said, unable to hold back my tears.

"What's wrong, Morgan? I'm okay. Don't cry. I'm better."

"I know, but I didn't think you were going to be okay. I've been mean about the situation all summer. Yesterday, when I wasn't sure if you were going to heaven or not, I just prayed. Now that I see you, it feels really good to hug you and hear how much you've missed me too. I'm sorry."

"Well, Morgan, you're growing up. I'm gonna have to tell your dad that he did a great job with you this summer. Do you want me to forgive you?"

"Yes. I think after all of this I know now that having a bad attitude gets you nowhere. I'm glad you have Mr. Derek. And he told me that he loves me too. Dad said before he left that Mr. Derek was a great guy and I should give him a chance."

"Yes, Morgan. He just wants you to love him too. You have such a big heart. Is it okay for you to love your two dads?"

Thinking really hard about her question so I wouldn't tell a fib, I said, "I can, Mommy."

"So how's your new school, baby? Do you like it? Did you make cool friends? Talk to me."

Before I could answer, Mama walked into the room. "Look who's here. It's a new little man who can't wait to see his mommy."

When Mama stepped aside, the nurse came in behind her, bringing the baby and smiling.

Mama grinned and said, "I couldn't wait to see my daughter's face when she's holding her precious baby boy."

Then the nurse placed the baby in Mommy's arms and said, "He can't stay long. I'll be back to get him in a few minutes."

Before she left, she helped me to put on a plastic gown and paper mask to cover my mouth. It felt like I was playing dress-up the way I sometimes do with Mama. After she explained that I had to wear it so the baby wouldn't get sick, the nurse walked out and closed the door.

Pretty soon I wanted to follow her and go back to the waiting area. As I sat there watching my mom and Mama playing with the tiny person, who was smaller than my dolls, I learned that my time was slipping away. They were laughing and very happy. With all of their *oohing* and *cooing*, it made me fold my arms and put a frown on my face.

I had seen the baby yesterday and was happy he was okay, but this was my time with my mom, and he was taking that away.

Mommy noticed my face didn't have a smile and told my grandmother, "Mom, I'm a little tired. I'm going to spend time with the baby later on. I want to have a moment with Morgan."

"Sure. I'm sorry, Morgan. Come on over here and talk to your mommy."

Just then, the nurse opened the door. In a minute, like a magician, she and that baby disappeared.

Mama kissed my mommy on the top of her head and left the room too. I turned around and looked out the window at all the cars that were on the street. Like Mama said, I needed to keep my mind on positive things so I wouldn't become sad or upset. Counting how many red cars and blue cars there were in the parking lot seemed more interesting to me than talking to my mom. After all, she ignored me when that little guy came in the room.

"Morgan, could you come over here, please? Don't be mad, baby. He's your brother. We have such little time together. Let's not waste it being mad. Please, baby, come over and sit with me. You are my heart and so is your new brother. Just like you have so much room in your heart to love so many, I do too. Don't ever feel like you have to compete with your brother for my love, my attention, or my time. Well, he is a baby so he might need more time, but—"

Blowing steam I said, "But what, Mom? Why did you have to have another baby? I guess that's what I wanted to ask you all summer. Why wasn't I enough?"

"You *are* enough, Morgan. But God gave me another surprise blessing. And that little boy is going to need his big sister. I'm counting on you to show him how to be smart . . . and how to care about others. He truly needs you."

"I'll try," I said. I could see this really meant a lot to my mom, and I didn't want to let her down.

"And when you do that, you're taking a huge step. Just try for me. We're gonna be a happy family, you'll see."

The kiss she planted on my forehead made me feel good again. I wasn't mad anymore and so I unfolded my arms. I guess having a new baby around wouldn't be such a bad thing.

● ● ● ● ●

The week had flown by and Mom was coming home from the hospital with the baby today. Mom told me that his name was Jayden. I thought they would name him Derek Jr., but Mr. Derek said that he wanted his son to have his own **identity**. I didn't know what that meant but the grown-ups told me that it meant the baby wouldn't have to try and be just like his dad. Mr. Derek wanted Jayden to make a fresh start with his own name.

It was Sunday and Mama and I were on our way to church. As much as I didn't want to go this morning, I knew once church was over, we were headed straight to see Mommy and Jayden. So I sat still for the moment and watched the clock while I waited.

I spent the time thinking about how much I loved my mommy and how much I missed her. She called me every day now that she was better. We both couldn't wait to see each other again.

"And the Scripture today is taken from Philippians 4:8, *Whatever is true, honorable, right, pure, lovely, and good, dwell or think, on these things.* What do you guys think that means?" Mr. Martin asked us in the Bible study class.

I had been in Mr. Martin's Sunday school class for about a year now. You have to stay in the same class for two years and then you can move. So when I go to third grade, I will be in a new class. Right now I'm the only second grader in the class and the rest are in the first grade. It's not that I know more than them, I'm just older.

"Does it mean, think about when you get up in the morning?" a boy named John asked.

"No, that's not what it means," Mr. Martin told him nicely.

"Good, because I don't like when my big brother has to wake me up and get me ready in the morning because my parents have to work."

"Okay, anyone else?"

"I know. It means, think about what you can get from the mall," said a girl named Kelly.

"No, that's not it."

She said, "Good. I didn't have new clothes for the first week of school and I got picked on."

A lot of kids in the class were mad about what they did and didn't get. And about what their parents did and didn't buy. But Mr. Martin kept telling them, "No." So I looked at him with puppy dog eyes, wanting him to explain to everyone what it meant. But he didn't notice me. After going through a week when I almost lost my mom, it made me love her and care about her a lot more.

Without waiting to be called on, I said, "That Scripture means we should think about God because He's so great. And He can do anything but fail."

"Wow, Morgan, that was a very good answer. Thank you," Mr. Martin said.

"Oh, she only knew that because some grown-ups told her," John chimed in.

I stood up and put both hands on my hips. "That's true, but I had to **experience** it myself. My mommy was just in the hospital, and we didn't know if she was gonna make it, but she did. God did that. We never know what He can do for us until we trust Him. So tell me why you're mad because you have to get up in the morning with your brother? At least you're blessed to see another day. And you, Kelly, why are you upset because you didn't get new clothes for school? Don't you already have some clothes? Be happy that your parents have a job. Be happy that you have parents. Be happy with what you have."

"Thank you, Morgan," Mr. Martin said, as he signaled for me to sit down. "What she is saying is that life is short, so don't take it for granted. We shouldn't think about things that make us sad and upset. What we should do is think about God and the things He does for us. He gave us life, and He sent His only Son to die on the cross for our sins."

Everyone was listening closely. Mouths were closed and ears were open. It felt good to share a life lesson with the group. I also listened real hard to Mr. Martin as he went on with his speech.

"It is good news to hear that John's parents have jobs. It is good news that Morgan's mom pulled through, but the true thing that should get us excited is that we have a risen Savior. That means He is a Savior who didn't stay buried. We should focus on that and be thankful because Jesus loves us so much that we'll have **everlasting** life."

Knowing that Jesus loves me that much was great news.

## Letter to Dad

Dear Dad,

Let me get to the great news. Mommy is okay.
Yeah! The baby is named Jayden. I'm **pretending** to
like him. It's nothing **negative** against him, it's just
me. I'm supposed to teach him **stuff**. Maybe one
day I'll teach him how to tell time and set Papa's
**mahogany** clock.

Oh and my class is acting better for our
teacher, Miss Nelson. Today we had no **distractions**.
At first I didn't like being called smart, but
now I am okay with my **identity**. You taught me to
learn from every **experience** I have in life, and I am
learning.

Sunday school was great. I learned that because
I believe in Jesus, I will have **everlasting** life.
Isn't that cool? Be safe there, Dad.

Your daughter,
Learning from life, Morgan

# Word Search

```
D G P M E G A T I V P E
P I O S A J S F D F R V
R D S B T H H O E F E E
E E E T R V O X N R T R
T N V K R A R G L I E L
E T I I Z A E D A E M A
N I T N I R C H K N B S
D T A D T H E T P D Y T
I Y G D I S T R I C T I
N P E M A H O G N O Y N
G J N C H I C A G O N G
P E X P E R I E N C E S
```

**DISTRACTIONS**

**EVERLASTING**

**EXPERIENCE**

**IDENTITY**

**MAHOGANY**

**NEGATIVE**

**PRETENDING**

# Words to Know and Learn

**1) pre·tend** (prĭ-tĕnd') *verb*
To give an appearance of something being true or real

**2) neg·a·tive** (nĕg'ə-tĭv) *adjective*
Not helpful; criticizing

**3) mahogany** (mə-hŏg'ə-nē) *noun*
Reddish brown color

**4) dis·trac·tion** (dĭ-străk'shən) *noun*
Something that takes attenion away

**5) i·den·ti·ty** (ī-dĕn'tĭ-tē) *noun*
The things by which an individual is recognized and known

**6) ex·pe·ri·ence** (ĭk-spîr'ē-əns) *noun*
An event or a series of events a person has gone through

**7) ev·er·last·ing** (ĕv'ər-lăs'tĭng) *adjective*
Something that will last forever; eternal

# Chapter 4
## Low Energy

"Morgan! Could you bring me a bottle out of the refrigerator for the baby, please?"

It wasn't bad that Mommy asked me to help her. But three minutes before she needed the bottle, she asked me to bring her a diaper. And before that, it was a bib. It seemed like every time I wanted to read a book, play with my dolls, or watch TV, I had to do something to help baby Jayden. I was getting used to being a big sister, but I wasn't happy to be an all-day big sister helper.

Just when I was dragging myself in the kitchen to get the bottle, the telephone rang. Mom yelled out, "Morgan, honey, grab the phone!"

At first, I didn't want to because I knew it was another person letting us know when they were coming over to see the baby. Mom and Jayden had been home for three weeks now and every day somebody was always visiting. There is more to the world than a newborn baby, people! And it was driving me crazy.

Everyone kept saying, "Oh, Morgan, you're so sweet to help your mom. Oh, Morgan, you're so blessed to have such a sweet baby brother." And I was getting more and more upset.

When I got to the phone this time, a smile came across my face when I saw the number. It was Brooke. *Finally, someone for me,* I thought.

"Hey," I said in a happy tone. It was as if speaking to her helped me to not be so mad about the way things were at home.

"I need some help with my homework, Morgan!"

"What homework? Do you mean the English homework page? That was easy. **Pronouns** are a blast."

"Yeah, easy for you maybe, but I don't even know what a pronoun is. Can you help me?"

"Did you look over the stuff Miss Nelson showed us in our English book?"

"I left my book at school. All I brought home was my homework notebook and this worksheet."

"Morgan!" Mom called out. "Bring me the milk, honey."

"I hear your mom looking for you. Can I just hold on until you come back and then you can help me?" Brooke asked in a helpless voice.

Now I was getting angry again! Brooke wanted me to help with her homework. Mommy kept calling me every two seconds. Jayden was eating every few hours. What was wrong with the boy, and why did he eat so much? He just had a bottle like an hour ago.

"Something must be wrong with his stomach. He won't stop eating," I said into the phone.

"He eats so much because he's going to be a man," I heard a boy's voice say.

"Is that Trey?" I asked. "Brooke, what is he doing on the phone?"

"He called me first to see if I knew how to do the worksheet and then I called you. We really need help, Morgan."

In a not-too-happy way, I huffed, "Can you hold on real quick? I need to see what my mom wants."

"See, Brooke. I told you she didn't know how to do it either," Trey said.

"Yes, I do. I'll be right back."

The three of us had gotten closer over the past few weeks. At school, we were on the same team so we had to work together on everything. Even though Brooke and Trey were always trying to be the best, they made the work harder. Miss Nelson would explain to us one thing and they would do another because they didn't listen to all of the directions. Now, I was here to save the day.

My mom had taught me how to warm the baby's bottle. Of course, she went behind me and checked to see if it was too warm for baby Jayden. So I was just a bottle warmer, not a bottle tester.

"Here you go, Mom. I'm on the phone," I said quickly

before trying to turn and leave her side.

"With who, Morgan?"

"Trey and Brooke from class. We're going over the English homework." I knew saying we were being **productive** would make her agree to let me talk.

"Okay. Well, don't be too long. Maybe when you come back we can read a story to the baby. Would you like that?"

"No, not really," I looked over at her and said.

"Okay, Morgan," Mom said, as she tried to make the baby feel better.

Jayden was screaming my ears off! I knew he was hungry, but he was out of control. So much noise was coming out of this little bitty thing and he wouldn't settle down. He was so **annoying**.

"Was I like this when I was a baby?" I asked my mom, hoping she would say no.

"No, sweetie. You were a calm baby. I don't know why your brother is so restless. It's just the way he is. Thanks for the milk. Go back to your friends, and let me know if you need any help."

"Yes, ma'am. But I hope Jayden stops crying so I can hear."

When I picked up the phone again, I could hear Trey and Brooke going back and forth about something. I just listened to them argue.

"No. The sentence is: 'They took us to the mall and out to dinner.' The pronoun is *they*, Brooke," said Trey.

"No, the pronoun is *us*," said Brooke.

I cut in and said, "Our homework said to underline the pronoun and double underline the subject pronoun. So both *they* and *us* are correct, but the subject pronoun is . . . I'm waiting because I want one of you to tell me the answer."

"Why don't you just tell us?"

"Okay, how about this. Who took us to dinner?" I asked.

"They did," Brooke answered. "So *they* is the subject pronoun."

"Correct. The next sentence is: 'We will have them over for dinner.' What are the pronouns?" I asked.

"I got this one," Trey said. "*We* and *them.*"

I said, "Yes! Now, what's the subject pronoun?"

"Let's see. Who will have them for dinner? The answer is *we,*" Brooke said.

"Very good, guys. So you double underline it. Y'all can do this if you use my little trick. Whenever I can put some-one's name in the sentence, it helps to spot the pronoun. Like, if the sentence is: 'He took her to the store,' I can say: 'Trey took Brooke to the store.' See, it really works."

Brooke was satisfied, so she changed the subject. "I'm so excited about Saturday," she said.

Then I told her, "I know, me too. I can't wait for my grandparents to take us out."

"Where are y'all going? I wanna go," Trey said quickly.

"We're going to a fancy restaurant. You wouldn't wanna come," I told him.

"But we're also going to a car show. Maybe he would want to go there," Brooke said. "And everyone thinks your grandparents are super nice."

"Oh yeah, your granddad is awesome. I can just hang with him all day. I'll behave at a fancy restaurant. I know how to **control** myself. I won't even be thinking about you girls."

"Then I'll ask Papa."

"It'll be fun, Morgan," Brooke said.

Getting away from my house was something I was excited about. Doing anything else would be better than being here. I was so tired of being the **errand** girl for Jayden. And I was tired of being errand girl to Mommy. Now it was my turn to have fun. Or at least I hoped so.

●  ●  ●  ●  ●

"No, no, Trey, that's my iced tea," Mama said. "Your glass is on your right."

Trey's eyes got real wide, like he knew he'd done something wrong. "Oh, I'm sorry, Mrs. Brundy."

Papa laughed and said, "That's okay, son. I've been doing this for years and I still can't get this table manners stuff down."

"Yes, we know," Mama said with a grin. "The three of you sit up straight. No slouching at the table. Brooke, elbows off. Morgan, you know that napkin is supposed to be in your lap."

Oh! I was so tired of hearing Mama's rules. My grandmother loved for us to go to fancy restaurants just so she could teach me the proper way of doing things. You'd think I'd almost have it down by now. Then again I was so tired from the baby waking me up at night. The way that he cried all the time, it's no wonder I didn't forget my own name.

Then Trey leaned over to my granddad. He thought he was whispering but we all heard him. "When I grow up, am I gonna have to take my girlfriend out to a fancy place like this? Will I be able to afford it?"

"That's exactly why you have to get a good education and a good job. Knowledge is money, son," Papa replied.

Trey looked around and smiled at the nice place. "Before I came here, I was just going to take my girl to Mickey D's like my big brother does," he said.

"I wouldn't wanna go to Mickey D's," Brooke said, rolling her eyes.

"I wasn't even talking to you," Trey shot back.

"Well, we're all eating here together, young man. No private conversations," Mama told him.

The restaurant was a very old building that had just been fixed up. It had a fresh garden outside, and you could see all the pretty **landscape**. We were given special orders not to touch the pretty china dishes. I guess they didn't want us breaking up their place.

The people around us didn't look much like us. Mama said African Americans came here a lot, but today we were the only ones. She wanted us to be on our best behavior so we wouldn't go around looking like Black folks with no home training. I remember overhearing Mama telling Miss May exactly that before we left.

"So, what are we going to talk about?" Papa asked.

"How about parents that work their children too hard," I said, showing how upset I've been by what had been going on at home.

"Yeah. I have to do most of the dishes at my house. My big sister and my brother are supposed to help me, but when my mom leaves they make me do all the work. And that's not fair," Brooke complained.

"I just wished my dad was around so that my mom wouldn't have to take on being the mother and father. She has to work so much," Trey added.

Papa said, "I understand, young man. Just like you were asking about what you need to do when it's time to date a young lady, you have to take care of things at home right now. Such things like taking out the trash and keeping your room clean are your responsibility. You can even help your older brother check the locks on the door before you go to bed. I'm sure your mom counts on you all."

"Well, I don't understand why we have to do chores. My sister says that kids aren't asked to be born and when parents have kids, they shouldn't make them do anything," Brooke added.

"Why not? That's not the way life is. If you never had chores you wouldn't learn how to take care of yourselves when you grow older. You'd be spoiled and never feel like you have to work for anything," Mama said, as she sipped her tea.

"What you guys have to realize is that parents aren't perfect, but that doesn't mean that they don't love you. They care about what you need, but sisters and brothers should help each other and their parents too. That way, life is better for all of us. Now eat up. We gotta go and check out some cool cars," Papa said.

I looked over at Brooke and Trey. "I got that. Did y'all get that?"

"I think I got that. Did you get that?" Trey asked, as we all laughed.

Then the waiter brought our dessert. We had a frozen fruit bar that didn't look good at first but it tasted really good.

Before we left the Swan Coach House, we walked through the museum that was on the other side of the restaurant. Seeing the paintings from the various artists made me think hard. Some paintings looked sad and some looked happy, but they were all showing how the artist was feeling. I wasn't much interested in art, but I do want to be a part of something important. It could be a chorus because I like to sing. Or even ballet, since I like to dance. I just want to do something to show that I am an artist too.

Staring at one of the paintings, I didn't even notice Brooke come up behind me. She was watching me and asked, "What are you thinking?"

"I'm not thinking anything except art makes you

express yourself. Looking at this stuff really makes me wanna tell my mom how much I do not like that baby."

"You know that will break her heart, right?"

While we were talking, Trey joined in. "Be happy that there's only one baby at your house. My mom is taking care of my brother's two kids and she has one of her own, so it's three little babies at my house."

"Being the baby isn't that great either. Everyone just pushes you around and makes you do what they want," Brooke said.

"I'm not a nice person," I huffed. "Because I don't care about what's going on at your houses. You guys don't have it nowhere near as bad as me."

Then Trey said something very important. "I don't know. Maybe you're right, Morgan. We might not have it as bad as you. But you're talking about telling your mom that you don't like her baby, and she might start not liking you."

My mouth dropped completely. Trey didn't even know what he said. Then Papa told us it was time to go. Brooke saw that I was upset and put her arm around me, trying to comfort me.

"It's gonna be okay," she told me. "But Trey is right. I really don't think you should tell your mom how you feel about the baby."

I heard them both and just dropped my head. I really didn't like the way I had been feeling. Why did I have to feel so down?

· · · · ·

Later that night, I couldn't sleep. All I kept hearing was, "Wahh! Wahh! Wahh!" The baby just wouldn't stop crying. I tried putting the pillow over my head and then I put the covers over my face. I even put cotton balls in my ears, but none of it helped. Mommy and Mr. Derek were taking care of Jayden, but whatever they were doing to the little ball of noise wasn't working.

Mr. Derek came out of the baby's room and saw me sitting on the floor in my room. "Morgan, get back in the bed, sweetheart."

"How can I go to sleep when the baby is making all that noise? Gosh! Why do we have to have a baby in the first place? No one in the house is happy with him. He's keeping us all up! Ugh!"

With tears in her eyes, Mommy came into the room with us. "Morgan, please! Don't do this right now. Something is wrong with Jayden. Mama is on her way over here to look after you while we take him to the hospital. I know he's annoying you, and I know he's keeping you up, but please pray for him to get better. Okay? See, Derek. That's why I feel like a horrible mother. I didn't even know something was wrong with my son or my daughter."

Mr. Derek went and took the baby from her. He held my mom and said, "No, no. It's not your fault. None of us knew something was seriously wrong with Jayden. The fever just hasn't broken in a couple of days. But once the doctor gives him some medicine he'll be fine, you'll see."

"But what if he's not fine? Morgan's right. See, you

haven't been here all day and he's been crying all day. This is all my fault," Mommy said through her tears.

I had never seen my mother so scared and it really made me worry. Why didn't I realize that Jayden wasn't feeling well? I'm smart, but I'd been so upset that he was taking over my world. I didn't even realize that maybe all he needed was for his big sister to love him and make it better. I knew something was wrong with him, and I wasn't doing my job. I just wanted him to be gone. And now, what if he left tonight and never came back?

"I wanna go to the hospital, too. We don't have to wait on Mama; just let me grab my shoes and we can leave right away," I said.

"No, I don't want you going to the hospital this late," Mom said.

"We don't need to waste any time getting the baby there. Let's take Morgan and go," Mr. Derek said to her.

Even though she agreed, as soon as we got to the door, Mama and Papa were there.

Trying to go around my grandparents, I said, "You guys don't have to stay here with me. I'm going to the hospital too."

"We're going to let your parents handle this, big girl. We'll stay here with you and wait by the phone." Papa lifted me into his arms and said, "Don't be upset. Baby Jayden will be fine."

Mommy and Mr. Derek took the baby to the hospital. I stood there watching until the car sped away. I felt just as bad as I did when I'd been mean to Mom.

When Papa led me to the living room, I said, "This is all my fault, Papa. You know how really sad I was when the baby came. I was so busy helping Mommy that it made me mad. Then everyone was coming over to see the baby and not me. I didn't want him to be here, and now he's sick. I'm so sorry." I couldn't stop crying.

"I know you learned a great lesson. Now didn't you, Morgan?" Mama said, sitting across from us on the loveseat.

"Yes. I think so."

"What lesson did you learn, Morgan?"

I took a deep breath to stop crying so hard, and said, "I learned that I should not spend my time being mad and that I was supposed to concentrate on good things. And I learned to never think bad about people because they won't always be here."

"That's good, baby girl. Remember too that human beings make mistakes," Papa said.

So he kept talking to me. "We're never going to be perfect until we leave this earth and live in heaven with Jesus. So I hope you also learned that jealousy, anger, and envy have no place in a little girl's world. Okay, so your brother got on your nerves. Okay, so your mom keeps bugging you to help her. Give all of that to God. You don't have to complain to your mom, your dad, your stepdad, your Mama, or me. God likes it when you talk to Him. That's why Jesus said in Matthew 11:30, 'My yoke is easy and My burden is light.'" He wants you to give your **burdens** to Him, Morgan.

"What does that mean?" I asked Papa.

He took my hand and said, "It means take your troubles to Him, and He'll make it all better. Try talking to Him right now."

"Okay, I'll try. *Dear Lord, I haven't been the nicest person. I know You forgave me about Jayden and my mom forgave me too, but she thinks that I don't love him. But I do love him, Lord. I was just upset, and I wasn't ready to be a big sister yet. I'm sorry. Please help my little brother. Thank You, Lord.*"

The next thing I knew I was closing my eyes and falling asleep next to Papa. It was great to talk about my feelings. It felt even better because I was giving it all to God. My heart was happy, and my eyes were heavy. On the inside, I prayed some more that the Lord would help me have a better attitude.

"Go ahead and put her to bed now," I heard Mama say, as I was being carried down the hall. "Our little grandbaby is always busy. Now she's tired and has low energy."

# Letter to Dad

Dear Dad,

School is cool still. We learned about **pronouns**. Examples of pronouns are: we, you, I, us, they, them, she, and he. I've been really **productive** because I helped my friends study.

I hope your day is better than mine. I made a big mistake. Baby Jayden was **annoying** me because he cried all the time. Turns out he is sick. Mom lost **control** and cried when they took him to the hospital. See I was tired of running **errands** for Mom and got mad at the baby. I know that was wrong.

I think about you in Africa and wonder how everything looks. Is the **landscape** over there nice? I pray you don't have many **burdens**. I need you to come home, Daddy.

                    Your daughter,
                    Trying to be better, Morgan

# Word Search

```
W  H  A  T  C  A  U  S  E  M  L  H
H  L  G  K  P  H  N  U  O  O  A  E
O  Q  N  V  R  U  W  H  R  H  N  L
W  U  I  F  O  X  C  T  W  E  D  P
H  B  Y  N  D  S  N  T  E  S  S  O
E  U  O  W  U  O  W  H  Y  H  C  T
R  R  N  H  C  T  H  E  O  E  A  H
P  D  N  O  T  H  O  Y  U  I  P  E
W  E  A  S  I  E  M  X  M  T  E  R
H  N  Z  E  V  M  T  H  O  S  E  S
Y  S  R  J  E  R  R  A  N  D  S  P
B  E  P  O  S  I  T  I  V  E  I  T
```

**ANNOYING**

**BURDENS**

**CONTROL**

**ERRANDS**

**LANDSCAPE**

**PRODUCTIVE**

**PRONOUNS**

## Words to Know and Learn

1) **pro·noun** (prō'noun') *noun*
The part of speech that is used as a substitute for nouns; he, she, it, him, her are examples.

2) **pro·duc·tive** (prə-dŭk'tĭv, prō-) *adjective*
Something that brings about useful results

3) **an·noy·ing** (ə-noi'ĭng) *adjective*
Irritating; bothersome

4) **con·trol** (kən-trōl') *verb*
To hold in restraint; check

5) **er·rand** (ĕr'ənd) *noun*
A short trip taken to do a task, usually for someone else

6) **land·scape** (lănd'skāp') *noun*
Scenery that can be seen from a single view

7) **bur·den** (bûr'dn) *noun*
Something that is emotionally difficult to bear

# Chapter 5
# Bright Spark

"Something sure does smell good, and I can't wait to eat it," I said, jumping from my bed. I like to eat good food, especially when it was Mama's cooking. So I **scrambled** around to find my robe and house slippers. I was hungry and ready to eat.

Then I remembered what happened last night. I knew it either had to be a bad dream or my little brother was really sick. Before I got sad again, I dashed to the kitchen looking for someone in the house to get my questions answered.

"Mama? Papa?" I called out not caring about the food anymore.

"We're in the kitchen, Morgan," Papa said.

When I walked through the door, Mama was standing at the stove turning over the bacon. Papa was taking the orange juice out of the refrigerator. To my surprise, when he closed the door, Mom and Mr. Derek were already seated at the table. Baby Jayden in his seat was making small noises and moving around like he was ready to eat.

"He's okay! He's okay!" I yelled because I was so happy.

"Yes, he is. And he can't wait to see you," Mommy told me.

I went over to his baby seat, and the little guy was smiling at me. His lips made a cute shape at me. "Hey, Jayden. Remember me? I'm Morgan, your big sister, and now that you're feeling better, I'm going to take extra good care of you." I looked at my mom. "So, Mommy what was wrong?"

"Well, the doctors said that he had a mild form of **colic**."

"What's that?"

"Some babies just get a pain in the tummy after they're born, and it makes them feel very uncomfortable and cranky. The formula I was giving him was too strong so we had to change it. Jayden has another appointment tomorrow, but he's fine, Morgan. Everything is okay."

"Morgan, would you like to go to my church today?" Mr. Derek asked me.

He was on staff at a new church and I had never been. Over the summer, I went to church with my dad. And since then I'd been going to church with my grandparents. Mommy and I were members there. I always knew he wanted me to go to his church, but for some reason I didn't want to, and no one made me go. But it was something about the way that he asked me. I knew he loved me and wanted me to be his little girl.

"Yes, I'm excited to go to your church," I replied. "Mama and Papa, are you going too?"

Mr. Derek said, "Please, come on. It'll be great to have you guys there."

Papa joked, "Well now, I wanna make sure your pastor can preach. I've been a member of Green Forest Baptist for over forty years, and I can't remember missing a Sunday. So if I'm gonna miss now, I want to make sure I get **spiritually** fed. I suppose I can check it out."

"Double Springs won't leave you hungry, sir," Mr. Derek said, as he chuckled. Mom looked over at her dad as if to say, *Daddy, hush.* Then she smiled.

After we had a large breakfast of grits, bacon, scrambled eggs, sliced fruit, and toast, Mama took the baby while my mom and I got ready.

"Hey, Morgan, come here and let me brush some of this gel in your hair."

"I love this stuff, Mom. It makes my hair shiny and pretty. Can you part it down the middle, please?"

"Sure, baby." Ten minutes later, I had two perfect ponytails with loose curls on the ends.

Then Mommy surprised me. Holding up a dress I'd never seen before, she said, "I thought you'd like to wear this today."

"A new dress? Why? I mean, it's beautiful." The dress

was a pretty cream color, and it was covered with ruffles and pearls.

I couldn't take my eyes off of it and asked her, "Why did you buy me a new one?"

"I just saw it in the store and knew it was for you. Let me show you what I'm wearing."

We walked over to her bed. A new cream colored suit was laid across her pillows. The sleeves had pearls lined around them and the skirt had ruffles at the bottom. It felt so special that our outfits looked **similar**.

"Mom! We're gonna be dressed alike, just like the old times."

"We're gonna do a lot of things we used to do, baby. I know you got a new dad and a new brother and a lot of things have changed. You had to settle into a new school too. But everything will be okay, I promise."

"School is great though, Mom. I've got two really cool friends."

"Yes, I know. Mama said they're nice kids. Trey, and what's the girl's name?"

I answered, "Her name is Brooke. They're both nice. We keep each other straight on everything. I didn't think I was gonna like it at this school, but I'm glad that I do."

● ● ● ● ●

Four hours later, church was over and I actually liked the service. In children's church, there were dancers around my age, and I liked how they danced. I watched them and wondered what it would be like to dance along with them.

When I saw Papa, I asked him how Rev. Barney preached.

"How was it, Papa? Did you get fed?"

"Sure did. He had a good message," Papa said, nodding his head.

When we were getting ready to leave, a girl that I saw in children's church came up to me. "Hi, I'm Sadie. Guess what, we're cousins."

"I don't have any cousins," I told her. "My dad's an only child and so is my mom."

"You're my uncle's new daughter."

Mr. Derek came over to us and said, "Morgan, I see you've met my sister's daughter. Sadie's in the third grade, her brother's in the fourth, and her sister's in the fifth. You two should get together sometime."

"That would be great," Sadie said. "My sister and brother get on my nerves, and it would be nice to have a cousin close to my age to hang out with."

We said our good-byes, and it was time to go.

"Okay, that sounds great. Well, I'll see you later," I told her.

I didn't know about her until then, but Sadie seemed really nice. My mom was hoping that we could get along. Seeing her happy made me happy. One thing we learned in children's church was that God wants good things for all of us. This summer when I wanted things to work out for me,

I didn't think it was gonna be like this. It is so much fun to learn that God really loves me.

* * * * *

I was a little late getting to school on Monday. I was too excited because Mom didn't make me ride the bus. She drove me so that she could meet my teacher. When we got there, the principal said it was fine for her to walk me down to my room.

Mom and Miss Nelson said hello and started chatting as soon as we walked into the room. I couldn't wait for her to meet Brooke and Trey.

But I was shocked to see the class was already in groups, and my two friends were sitting with a boy named Harold.

"You guys didn't save me a seat?" I asked them.

Trey said, "We didn't know if you were coming."

Not to be mean or anything, but Harold was the slowest kid in our class. Everyone else was smart, but it took Harold longer to answer a question before he got it right. Each group got points when they finished their work in a timely manner and, of all the kids, they chose Harold!

"Do you guys wanna meet my mom?" I asked Brooke and Trey.

"Can't you see we're working?" Brooke said. "We can wave at her and stuff, but we're trying to finish our worksheets."

"That's easy," I said, looking down at her paper. It was

a **preposition** worksheet and I just started giving Brooke the answers.

"*In the room* . . . is the first one. *Under the bed* . . . is number two. There's a preposition in number three too, it's . . . *across the bridge.*"

"Well, you might wanna go and get your own sheet and do it," Brooke told me. "We don't need your help."

"Yeah, we don't need your help," Trey said, repeating what she just said.

I walked away from their table and went back over to my mom with teary eyes. With a smile on my face, I tried to pretend so that she couldn't see I was sad and my heart was hurting.

When I walked over to them, Mom was saying good-bye to my teacher.

"Don't you want me to meet your friends now, Morgan?"

Holding my head down, I replied, "No. Not today."

"Morgan, why don't you walk your mom outside. Then come back in to start your work. Your mom can meet your friends another time." Miss Nelson seemed to notice that there was something else going on.

"Yes, ma'am."

"What's wrong, baby?" Mom asked when we were outside in the hallway. "You were super excited this morning to get to school. What happened?"

All of a sudden, I couldn't hide how upset I was. So I said, "I don't know what's wrong with them! They were mean to me and didn't want me to help them. They always want me to go over the lesson with them. I really don't know what I did."

"It's okay, sweetie. Maybe when you guys go out for recess you can ask them about it. Don't worry. I'm sure everything will be okay. Sometimes we don't know when we hurt somebody or have done something to them, but we have to make sure to find out what the problem is. And most of the time, things can be worked out. You just make sure to have a great day today, okay? Kisses?" She bent down and kissed me on my cheek before walking out of the school.

As I watched her leave, Mom turned and blew me a kiss. Then she was gone, and I wanted to leave with her.

I was alone for most of the day. And when it was time for recess, Miss Nelson asked me to stay inside.

"Morgan, you are very smart. So far, you've scored 100 percent on all of your tests. You've proven that you can do second grade work. Now, I've been talking with the other teachers and we think it would be a good idea to go ahead and skip you to the third grade. You've got a lot of potential, and that could help you grow and blossom even faster."

She wanted me to think about it because she saw the idea as a good thing. But I didn't. It scared me so bad because I wasn't ready to move up yet. Somehow it felt like I was watching a scary movie with my dad and had to stop in the middle of it.

"No, I don't want to move. I like the grade I'm in. I'm not ready to go ahead."

Miss Nelson wasn't finished trying to encourage me.

"Everyone thinks you're **exceptional**. I spoke to your mom briefly today, and we plan to meet with her next week. The principal and I were talking about the idea this morning, and she gave her stamp of approval. So, before you say no, take this letter home to your mom so you both can talk it over. Then we'll decide."

I took the letter from her and just stared at it. Was I supposed to feel better to know that I might be leaving my friends and going to another grade? I knew I wasn't ready to handle the third grade. But I was ready to go to recess. When I walked onto the playground, I went right over to Brooke. She looked at me and turned the other way.

"Okay," I said to her, **refusing** to go away. "Be honest. If you have a problem with me, tell me. You're my friend, and I care about you. I didn't do anything to you, Brooke. Now, if Trey wanted to stop talking to me, then I'd get over it because he's just a boy. But I thought we were becoming best friends. You said you were praying for me. Why did that change?"

"I don't know," she said. "Why should it matter to you anyway? When you go to your new grade, you're just gonna forget about us. Why do you wanna hang out with me?"

"How did you know I was going to another grade?"

"We all heard the principal talking to Miss Nelson this morning. 'Morgan's so smart. She should be around kids that are more on her level. Morgan is the best . . . ,'" Brooke said in a mocking voice.

"So, I guess that means if you're somebody's best

friend you don't want good things to happen to them? You don't want other people to think they're cool?"

Brooke dropped her head. She couldn't even look at me because she knew I had a good point. It didn't seem right for her to be jealous of me. But I couldn't be mad at her. I've been jealous before too, so I went to her and put my arms around her. Being jealous was not a good feeling to have on your heart.

"You know, I was jealous of my brother, Jayden, and I was jealous of my new dad too. Lately, I've been jealous a lot, so I understand. But my Papa told me to look at myself and give those things to God. I just want to ask you to do the same. I care about you, Brooke, and I know you care about me. We can have the best friendship in the world and it doesn't matter if I'm in the second or the third grade. If we're buddies, then we're buddies. But you have to wanna be my buddy too. Mama always says to me, it's in your hands now. So you decide."

● ● ● ● ●

Mr. Derek was taking me on a play date with his nieces and nephew. We went to a bowling alley that had bumper cars, an arcade, and laser tag. I had never played laser tag before, but I heard it was fun. So I couldn't wait to put on cool gear and run around in the dark, trying to tag other people. The team that hit their target with the most points would win the game.

Sadie's sister, Samantha, was much older than me. And

she was the coolest! Samantha wanted people to call her Sam for short. She never told me why, but I just did it. Her hair looked so pretty, and her clothes were cool. Her nails had cute designs on them too. She was a girly girl, and I'm a girly girl too. I really liked her look a lot. When I get to the fifth grade, I hope I'll still be a girly girl and be like her.

But Drake was so bossy. Trying to run everything, he said, "Let's go play basketball first. After that, I wanna get on the bumper cars and then play laser tag." The whole time, Drake kept saying what he wanted to do, over and over again. He was really getting on my nerves.

Finally, Mr. Derek said, "We're going to play laser tag together. We already did some things you wanted to do, Drake."

Sadie, Mr. Derek, and I were on the same team. Sam and Drake were on the other. With Mr. Derek on our team, we beat them, and it was so much fun. Sam said it was because we had Uncle Derek. Maybe it was. Maybe it wasn't. But it was great that he could be so cool. As we ran through the maze, he helped me out. When it was too dark and I couldn't see my enemies, I knew he had my back.

While Sam, Drake, and Mr. Derek went to ride on the bumper cars, Sadie said, "Morgan, you know you got a good dad, right?"

"I'm learning."

"Yeah. Our mom told us that he didn't think you liked him too much. We wanted to meet you sooner, but he said you weren't ready."

We didn't know each other that well, but Sadie didn't waste any time telling me how she felt. That was great! I could tell she was a good person. She was standing up for her uncle because she loved him. I would have done the same thing for Mama, Papa, Mommy, Daddy, and baby Jayden.

"Morgan, Uncle Derek's not bad, but I can see how it can be hard if your parents aren't together. My dad died when I was two. Uncle Derek does a lot with us. He's great. We're always able to talk to him about anything. Maybe that's just the way he is; or because he's a minister, that's the reason he knows how to help people. I can tell you that he's awesome, and you're blessed to have him."

Being honest with her, I said, "I guess because I already have a dad, I didn't know that having two of them could be even more fun."

"So, now do you think you could use two? Isn't your dad in the Navy on a ship far away from here?"

I squinted my eyes because I couldn't believe that she knew all this stuff about me. "You really know a lot about me," I said.

"I do. Like I told you, I always wanted to meet you. Sam's getting older, and she doesn't have time to spend with me anymore. It'll be fun to have a cousin so I can show you the ropes and how things are supposed to be. Besides, I don't want my uncle to be hurt. If you're not going to accept his love, then he needs to know now so he can stop trying and give all his love to me! No, not really,

I'm just playing," Sadie said playfully, as she pretended to punch me in the arm.

There was one slice of pizza left on the table and Sadie and I both wanted more to eat. We just looked at each other but that wasn't going to make more pizza come to the table.

Drake growled at me. "You need to tell Uncle Derek we want more pizza."

"I can't tell him that. He's your uncle, you tell him," I said. I wasn't going to let Drake think he was the boss of me.

Sadie pushed me toward him and said, "And he's your dad, so go ahead."

"But I don't know how to tell him."

"Just tell him. Wouldn't you tell your other dad?"

"Yeah, I would."

"Okay. Then think of your stepdad as your dad too. Now go tell him."

I walked over to Mr. Derek and said, "May I ask you something?"

"Sure, Morgan. What's up?" he said, smiling at me.

"How are we going to work on this daddy and daughter thing?" I asked.

"By spending time together like this. I hope you're having fun. Is there anything else you want to know or ask me?"

Taking a deep breath, I did want to ask him something more important than about getting another pizza. "Sadie said you really love me. I think that you do too, but I want to know if you do. It's not like you ever said it."

He smiled again as we sat down on a nearby bench. "I love you. I love you because you are your mother's daughter, and I love her. I love you because you are your brother's sister, and I love him. And, most of all, I love you because you're you. Being the sweet girl that you are, I see how much you care about the world and want everything to be right."

Then Mr. Derek wanted to say something funny to me. "Besides, your dad made me promise I would take care of you, and I wouldn't think of letting him down. He's a naval officer, and he would show me that he isn't happy with me if I do. And we don't want that, now do we?"

I giggled, thinking about what Mr. Derek said about my daddy. Then what he said sank in . . . he really loves me! Wow!

"Morgan, I'd love for you to call me Daddy Derek. Would that be okay?"

I didn't know how to answer him.

Mr. Derek quickly looked away, but I wasn't sure why. I didn't mean to hurt his feelings. I just didn't know what to say.

Then he let me off the hook by saying, "You don't have to give me an answer right now. Is there anything else you want?"

"Yeah, more pizza!" I said, as I looked over at the gang. But I was still feeling bad inside.

"No problem. And, next time make those jokers ask me." We both laughed.

"Thank you," I said, as I hugged him real tight.

"What was that for?" he asked. "For giving you more pizza?"

I said, "For loving my mom, for giving me a new brother, for caring about me . . . and for buying us more pizza!"

"No problem. I've got a lot of things going on in my life, Morgan. But please know that you're one of the most important. To me, you're a bright spark."

## Letter to Dad

Dear Dad,

Today was really busy. I am sure you are busy too. I **scrambled** around to make sure that I got everything done. I'm still helping Mommy with Baby Jayden. He is better. The doctor said he had **colic**. I've been going to a new church and it's been **exceptional**. Mr. Derek is on **staff** at the church. And Papa said the preacher there is good and gets everyone **spiritually** fed. He wants me to call him Daddy Derek now. I'm thinking about it, but you were right. He loves me, and the more I get to know him, the more I see he is very **similar** to you. Oh yeah, my teacher has asked me to move up a grade. I don't know. Mommy and I are thinking it over. I do like school. This week we worked on **prepositions**. Be safe <u>in the woods</u>, <u>on the water</u>, and <u>under the bridge</u>. I love you, Daddy. I am **refusing** to be mad that you are not with me. I know that you are doing a great thing. I just miss you.

Your daughter,<br>Growing up, Morgan

# Word Search

```
D  B  A  Z  E  D  S  H  A  T  E  S
E  G  E  L  R  E  T  J  S  Y  X  P
L  S  G  O  O  L  E  O  I  E  C  E
I  T  N  X  S  B  L  Y  M  C  E  C
V  I  I  N  B  M  E  R  I  Z  P  I
E  L  S  A  Y  A  M  L  L  M  T  A
R  L  U  S  W  R  O  D  A  P  I  L
Y  S  F  H  T  C  A  R  R  X  O  M
P  R  E  P  O  S  I  T  I  O  N  D
D  I  R  P  R  A  Y  I  N  G  A  L
E  S  P  I  R  I  T  U  A  L  L  Y
K  S  A  Y  L  S  U  O  I  R  E  S
```

**COLIC**

**EXCEPTIONAL**

**PREPOSITION**

**REFUSING**

**SCRAMBLED**

**SIMILAR**

**SPIRITUALLY**

# Words to Know and Learn

**1) scram·ble** (skrăm'bəl) *verb*
To move or climb hurriedly, especially on the hands and knees

**2) col·ic** (kŏl'ĭk) *noun*
A condition of unknown cause seen in infants less than three months old, marked by periods of inconsolable crying lasting for hours at a time for at least three weeks

**3) spir·i·tu·al** (spĭr'ĭ-chū-əl) *adjective*
Of, from, or relating to God

**4) sim·i·lar** (sĭm'ə-lər) *adjective*
Showing a likeness in quality

**5) prep·o·si·tion** (prĕp'ə-zĭsh'ən) *noun*
A word put before a noun or pronoun to show how it is related to another word, such as, at, by, with, from

**6) ex·cep·tion·al** (ĭk-sĕp'shə-nəl) *adjective*
Well above average; extraordinary

**7) re·fuse** (rĭ-fyūz') *verb*
To not be willing to do or say something

# Chapter 6
# Outgoing Kid

"**So, you're telling** me that I get to go to work with you today, Papa?" I asked my granddad when we were on the way to his job.

"Yep. You always said you wanted to see what I do. Are you ready?"

"Yes, sir! I am! Do I get to drive the train too?" I raised my hands and acted like I was driving.

"What? No, baby, you're too young to run the train; I can't even let you get on. I could lose my job. And you don't want that to happen, do you?" he said.

"No way," I said in a loud voice. I would never want to be the cause of my Papa not working.

"I know you don't, pumpkin," he said. "The biggest thing I want you to learn about is that the **conductor** of a train is important for two reasons."

"Why, Papa? Tell me."

"When you go to a store, do you ever wonder how the products get there? Do you ever wonder who brings them?"

"I already know. The big eighteen-wheeler trucks bring them. We pass them all the time on the road. Some stuff comes in Mack trucks too."

"Okay, that's true, but do you know who brings the products to the truck people?"

I shook my head, having no clue. "I don't know."

"Well, the train takes them from where the stuff is made to the trucks. Then the trucks come and take them to the stores. Does that make sense?"

"I think so. You're saying if somebody doesn't bring the stuff to the truck **headquarters**, we won't be able to buy anything from the store?"

"Exactly, Morgan. So my job is important because I have to transport things from one place to another so that people can buy them, use them, and have a great day because they got what they need."

"That is important, Papa."

"I told you so. And secondly, I'm a 'pick-me-upper' kinda person."

"A 'pick-me-upper' kinda person? What is that?"

"Well, life is hard. Little lady, you understand that. You've seen your parents go their own ways. Now your dad is **overseas** serving our country. You had to go to a new school and make new friends."

"They don't like me anymore," I said. I looked out the

window, remembering Brooke and Trey telling me to stay out of their way.

"It might be bad because they don't like you. But it could be because they have something going on with them."

"I don't know what you mean."

Even though I loved talking to Papa, I was lost. He was so cool, and he always knew the right things to say. Brooke and Trey were mad at me, and I wished I could put them out of my mind. It was bothering me, and I didn't know what to do about it. But Papa was here to save the day. I listened closely because I wanted him to say something to help.

"Morgan, it means that maybe they aren't happy with who they are, and they take it out on you. In that case, they're taking it out on the wrong person. But a real friend, a person who has God in their heart, tries to help when the other person has problems. That person waits and prays for the friend to work on what's bothering them and feel better about themselves."

"Papa?"

"Yes, baby?"

"I really don't know what you mean," I said. It was kind of getting me angry.

But then I got excited when I saw all the trains at the yard. We were getting close to his job and I couldn't wait to get out of the car. There was no more time to talk then. We had to jump out of our car and grab our stuff to get through security. Papa had to clock in, and I was right at the yard office behind him. People were saying hello to me that I didn't even know, but they knew me. I **figured** Papa had told them all about me.

"Oh, is this Morgan? She is so precious! We saw your pictures in your granddad's office, and you are even prettier in person," one lady told me.

"Thank you," I said back. I was happy that my granddad loved me so much that he showed people my pictures, and they knew my name. We left the lady so Papa could talk to his boss, Mr. Joe.

"Hey, Mr. Joe," Papa said, but Mr. Joe barely spoke two words. He didn't even look up to see that Papa had an extra person with him. So I didn't say anything, I just stood behind Papa.

"You're usually here five minutes before your shift. One more minute and you would've been late," Mr. Joe said, in a mean tone.

Papa reached down, put his arm on Mr. Joe's shoulder and said, "I know it's been hard losing your wife. You even said yourself that you're glad she's not in pain anymore. You and I both know that she was in a tough battle, but I know she's in heaven. And that should make you smile."

Mr. Joe started smiling. He looked up with tears in his eyes and said, "Thank you. I needed to hear that. It's been hard. Who's that behind you?"

I moved to Papa's side.

"I didn't know we had company," Mr. Joe said, wiping his eyes.

"I'm not company, I'm family," I said, trying to be the nice girl my mom raised me to be.

"Well, we're glad to meet you at last. Are you going to see where your granddad works?"

"Yes, sir."

"He's a good man. I can tell by your smiling face that you're going to take good care of him. Have fun."

"Thank you, sir," I said, reaching out to shake his hand.

Papa pointed out different kinds of freight cars and told me what can be transported in each. As a conductor, he knows what is in each car and where it needs to go.

Once he sends a train on its way, it might take its load and drop off goods at many places. I was so thrilled to see Papa's work from his perspective. I smiled and told Papa I was proud he had such an important job.

Papa said, "You have such a sweet smile, Morgan, and I don't want you to lose that. You have this gift to make people happy."

"Like you did for Mr. Joe?" I asked.

"Yeah, just like that. That's what you need to show to your friends. Be nice to them even though they're giving you a hard time."

"I'll keep that in mind, Papa." Like grandfather, like granddaughter. It was a wonderful day. Choo-choo!

• • • • •

Later that evening, my grandmother was having a special sister meeting at her house. From what I heard her and my mom talking about, Mama was a chapter president of some group called Beta Gamma Pi. I think it was a group she joined in college. It's called a sorority. I didn't know what they did in a sorority, but I could tell it was important to Mama.

The house looked beautiful. Flowers were all over the living room where her sisters were going to sit. Her china was set on the dining room table, and the house smelled so good! I heard Mama ask Papa to go and visit with his friend or watch TV in the basement because she needed to focus on getting everything ready for her company.

Mama was acting a little nervous when she said, "Morgan, are you going to help me, or are you going with your granddad? I need to fix my hair and get dressed . . . oh no, something is wrong with my stove. My quiche didn't come out right."

"Ain't nothin' wrong with that stove," Papa joked. "You probably kept it in there too long."

When she didn't answer him back, I could tell that Papa was right. Mama was working too hard, and I knew exactly what she needed: a little helper assistant. "I'll help you, Mama."

I started by convincing Papa to go out of the house and head next door to visit his friend. Before leaving, he grunted worse than a hungry pig. "I hope this meeting don't last too long. I'm tired, and it's time for my dinner. You know I just got home from work."

Mama snapped, "You knew a month ago I had this meeting coming up, so I don't even wanna hear it."

After pushing Papa out the door, I turned to Mama. Ready to be her helper, I asked, "Okay, Mama, what do you want me to do?"

"Let's see," she said, scratching her head as she looked around the messy kitchen.

But every time she said I could do something, she did it herself. She was cooking, cleaning, and **stressing** all at the same time. She took some glasses out of the dishwasher to set them on the table for her guests. Without her telling me, I just started helping. Then when she walked around the table, I noticed something yellow and gushy on the floor. Before I could yell out, she slipped on the banana peel. The three glasses flew out of her hands, hit the floor, and broke into a million pieces.

"Oh, dear! Nothing is going right today," Mama said. She sounded as though she was having a pity party, like when kids get frustrated because they don't understand their homework.

"Don't worry. It'll get better, Mama. I'm just glad you didn't fall and get hurt."

"Thank you, baby," she said a little calmer.

Just then the phone rang and she went to answer it. So I grabbed the broom from the pantry. I knew I wasn't supposed to touch the broken glass, but the least I could do was sweep it all in one place for her to pick up the pieces.

All of a sudden, I heard a loud bump like she had hit

the table. "What! You can't come? But you have a big report that you're supposed to read. All right, all right," she said before she hung up the phone.

I watched Mama shake her head. "If it's not one thing it's another. Morgan, I'm coming. Be careful not to hurt yourself on that glass."

"Yes, ma'am," I replied, extra polite.

When I asked if I could have a taste of her punch, Mama wasn't too upset to say it was okay.

"Ewww, this is too sour!"

"Come on, Morgan. Nobody wants a bunch of sweet Kool-Aid." She came over to taste it herself. "Oh, boy. It does need a little more sugar. This really isn't good, and everyone will be here in a few minutes. What am I going to do?"

I grabbed her hands and thought about what Papa had said. A part of being a good person is making another person feel good. Mama was always there to make me feel special about something good, and she taught me how to forget about something bad. Now it was my turn to make her day. This meeting was really important to her, and someone needed to let her know it was going to be okay.

"Mama, you're a **leader**. Your cooking is the best. The house is so pretty. Those ladies are smart because they made you their president. I don't know what it is that you do, but it must be pretty important."

"We help make the community a better place, Morgan. We help people that can't help themselves."

"That is important, Mama. So your meeting is going to

go great because it's not just for you guys. You all are coming together to make other people feel safe and happy. If you gave them potato chips and popcorn, they would be happy. But you don't have to worry. You've got the kind of good food that Papa loves so much."

"Yes, and I'm going to fix him a plate so that he'll have some too. I see what you're trying to do. You're telling me to relax, aren't you?"

I nodded my head. "You've done everything else, Mama. It's about time you start getting dressed. Don't worry. I can greet the people as they come in, and then I'll go upstairs and read my book. But first, while you sweep up the glass that I moved over to the side, I'll add some more sugar to the punch."

"But don't put in too much," Mama said, shaking her finger at me. Then she smiled and told me, "Morgan, you're an angel."

"I'm just like you."

Helping to calm her down made me feel better than when I get a new doll. If being in a sorority was so good, maybe one day I'd be in one. But for now, I know that's what being a good Christian is about. I can't wait to tell my daddy! I hope he's safe. In my heart I know he'd be proud of me helping others just like he does.

●　●　●　●　●

"A jewel? Why do I have to wear a robe and be a jewel?" Daddy Derek's nephew, Drake, asked. "I don't wanna stand at the door and smile all morning."

We were learning how to be helpers and to take up money at church. Drake was complaining already and we hadn't even started being ushers.

Miss Floyd, the lady over our program, was telling us how important our job is. We will be the first faces that people see when they come into church.

The blue robes with the red bow in front were adorable. Only I could see how maybe a boy wouldn't think so. But I thought it was cool.

Then Miss Floyd gave us each a place to stand by the door. An older lady came in with her cane and, all of a sudden, her Bible and purse fell out of her hand. I ran over and picked them up for her. "Oh, baby. You don't know how much of a blessing this is. Thank you."

"You're welcome. Do you need help to your seat?"

She smiled and said sweetly, "No, thanks. What's your name?"

"I'm Morgan. What's yours?"

"I'm Miss Blue. The sun usually shines in my heart all day, but today my bones are tired. I didn't think I was gonna make it to church this morning, but, praise God, I'm here. It's such a blessing."

"Well, I'm glad to see you."

"Sugar, I'm glad to be in the house of the Lord. Now, you enjoy being a little girl. Time is precious, and it goes quickly. But you're serving and smiling for the Lord, and that's a good thing."

As it got closer to the time for church to start, more and more people were coming in. Some of them had a frown on their face, but it changed when I smiled at them. And once they were smiling they were nicer to the people around them. I hoped that just by me saying hello it helped everyone to have a better day. I was learning something very important. When I have a better attitude, it makes me feel better about things.

I saw Drake with his back turned, not speaking to people. Miss Floyd wasn't around to get him straight, but he wasn't about to get away with it. I went over to him and said, "You can't do that, Drake. You know what Miss Floyd told us. It's not right."

"Who says I can't? My uncle says I have to do this, but he didn't say I have to like it. I can do it my way," Drake said, as he shoved me.

I was getting madder at him, and I said a little louder, "Don't you know that you're not only standing up for my dad because this is where he works, but you're also standing up for God, our heavenly Father?"

"Wow! Morgan." Sadie heard me talking to her brother and came up to us. "You said dad, not stepdad or Daddy Derek. You called him dad. Do you think of my uncle as your dad now?"

"I don't know. It just slipped out, I guess."

"You *can* have two dads, you know. It's not a crime."

I just walked back over to my post and prayed, "Lord, I guess I'm blessed because You sent me two dads. I just don't wanna let my father down by calling someone else daddy."

"You don't have to call me daddy if you don't want to," a voice said behind me.

I turned around quickly and didn't even know that anyone else could hear me praying. "But, I do want to. I love you and my mom and Jayden. I think it's okay to have two dads."

He hugged me and said, "Just know that it doesn't have to be something that you do. The way you work hard at being an usher makes me proud to be your father. The Lord expects for us to bring all our cares and concerns to Him, to care about other people, and to love Him with our whole heart. I see you doing your best to do that, Morgan. I'm so happy you're my little girl."

I hugged him real tight. With two great dads to follow, I'm going to really work hard to be the best me I can be. I can't mess up. I want to be their outgoing kid.

## Letter to Dad

Dear Dad,

Papa showed me what a **conductor** of a train does. I met his boss at the company **headquarters**. I wished you were not **overseas** so that you could have seen it too. In the envelope is a picture of me and Papa near the train. One of his friends took it, and I **figured** you'd like to see it. Though I miss you, my **perspective** on you being gone is that you are blessing many people. So I will **stop stressing** about your safety. You are a **leader**, and I know you can take care of yourself and our country.

> Your daughter,
> Missing you, Morgan

# Word Search

```
T  H  O  R  S  E  Y  S  W  Z  J  R
P  E  R  S  P  E  C  T  I  V  E  A
C  A  P  T  A  I  N  R  T  C  N  I
A  D  B  R  E  D  A  E  L  O  G  L
U  Q  E  H  S  A  Y  S  C  N  I  R
W  U  T  R  H  V  O  S  O  D  N  O
A  A  H  D  U  E  L  I  N  U  E  A
G  R  E  E  K  G  F  N  D  C  D  D
O  T  Y  W  H  O  I  G  U  T  R  S
N  E  C  I  W  S  T  F  C  R  T  R
W  R  D  T  H  E  M  K  T  R  I  C
E  S  A  E  S  R  E  V  O  V  M  K
```

**CONDUCTOR**

**FIGURED**

**HEADQUARTERS**

**LEADER**

**OVERSEAS**

**PERSPECTIVE**

**STRESSING**

# Words to Know and Learn

**1) con·duc·tor** (kən–dŭk'tər) *noun*
One who is in charge of a railroad train, bus, or subway car

**2) head·quar·ters** (hĕd'kwôr'tərz) *noun*
A place where a company is located

**3) o·ver·seas** (ō'vər–sēz', ō'vər–sēz') *adverb*
Beyond the sea; in another country across the sea; abroad

**4) fig·ured** (fĭg'yərd) *verb*
To decide or assume that an idea is correct

**5) per·spec·tive** (pər–spĕk'tĭv) *noun*
A view or outlook over a certain area

**6) stress·ing** (strĕs–ing) *verb*
Putting mental, emotional, or physical strain or tension on one's self

**7) lead·er** (lē'dər) *noun*
One who has influence or power

# Chapter 7
## Much Charm

"Now, I've asked three times. Someone had better step up. Who will help Chanté understand what **adverbs** are?" Miss Nelson asked the class.

No one raised their hand. When I looked around the room and over at Chanté, her eyes were getting big and teary like a girl stuck in the rain. I never knew what it felt like not to have friends. In preschool, I had lots of friends, and in kindergarten and first grade I had a bunch of friends too.

The beginning of the year started off pretty cool after I stopped having an attitude. Brooke and Trey were my buddies. We studied together, did work together, and hung out. Then some weeks back they stopped being my friends. They said it was because I was getting a lot of attention from teachers and the principal.

After I talked to my family about it, I didn't let it bother me anymore. I think I had become **immune** to it. When my old friends started laughing at me, I didn't pay attention to them. But it bothered me to see Chanté all alone. Nobody wanted to help her, so I raised my hand faster than a racehorse trying to win a race.

"Morgan, will you help her?" our teacher asked.

"Yes, ma'am," I said.

"I will give you girls ten minutes to go over the lesson and then you can meet the rest of the class outside for recess."

When we were alone, Chanté wiped her eyes and looked away. It seemed like she was trying to hide, but I already saw she was sad. "You don't have to help me, you know," she said, still not looking at me.

"But I wanna help," I said to her. "Adverbs are easy and you'll get this. An adverb is a word that describes a verb. It's a word that tells how you do something. And there's a big trick to spotting them."

"What's the trick?"

"Well, most of the time adverbs end in *ly*."

"Really?"

"Yeah. So you look at the first sentence: 'The car was driving slowly.' Then you ask yourself: How was the car driving?"

I pointed to the word that ended in *ly* and started with an *s*.

"Slowly!" Chanté was already catching on.

"You got it, girl! Let's go to sentence number two: 'The

girl spoke softly into the microphone.' "

"Is it *softly*?" Chanté looked at me and asked.

"Yep. Now, you find the next adverbs in the rest of the sentences."

Chante read the last three sentences and worked fast. When she finished, she put her pencil down and said, "You're a great teacher. That's why you're so smart."

"I'm not that smart, I just like to learn. My dad is in the Navy on a ship by Africa serving our country. He taught me a lot. But you probably didn't wanna know all of that, did you?"

"No, it's okay. I think it's messed up how people treat you. We should all be real nice to you. Your dad is making sure we're all safe. We all owe you some **gratitude**. Some people in this class just like being mean," Chanté said.

"I never thought about it like that. My dad is helping our country. But what does that have to do with me? I don't want people to think that they have to give me any-thing. Well, to be honest, I liked it when I had friends. And I never want to be rude to anybody."

"It's like when you wanted to help me learn my adverbs. And the first thing I said was you don't have to."

"Nobody wants to make someone be their friend, you know?"

"Yeah," Chanté said. "You're really cool, Morgan. I guess I just can't believe I didn't take the time to get to know you sooner. I'm not funny, and I don't always know the cool things to say. I'm quiet, and people don't give me a chance."

"I've tried to come over to you a couple of times when I saw you sitting by yourself, but you always walked away. I thought you were telling me to just go away."

"No, I didn't even think you were coming up to me. I'm not used to having friends," she said.

"Well, let's talk. I already told you about my dad in the Navy. My mom got married again, so now I have a new dad. He works at our church. I also have a new baby brother named Jayden. I've been thinking lately about what Jesus would do. Sometimes I don't feel good, but I know He wants me to smile. I just think about Him and all the things He's blessed me with. And before I know it, the day is over. It doesn't even bother me if I hung out with anyone or not."

"Wow. Morgan, do you mind if I get your number, and call you sometime? You know, for homework and stuff."

I wrote it on a piece of paper. "Here's my number and you can give me yours. We can be friends."

"I'd love that!" she said, smiling.

It made me feel really good that she was happy to be my friend. But she wasn't the only one who was excited. I wasn't worried that Brooke and Trey weren't my friends anymore. I just prayed to God about it. Now, look at my blessing. God brought me somebody else to be my friend. My mommy is teaching me to leave stuff in His hands.

● ● ● ● ●

Over the next four days, during lunch, during breaks,

and during recess, Chanté and I had fun hanging out. She was learning about me, and I was learning about her, and we liked the cool things about each other. Chanté said her brother is one year older than her. She also told me that she lives with her brother and her mom. I don't know the story on her dad, and I didn't ask either.

"My mom can't wait to meet you," I said to Chanté. "She said maybe over the Thanksgiving break your mom can bring you over to my house."

"Oh, I would love that so much!" Chante squealed, almost making me deaf. Then she quickly got super calm and said, "Someone wants to talk to you."

I turned around to see Brooke standing behind me. I wasn't sure how long she'd been there. Since she didn't even say excuse me, I didn't know she was there at all.

"You need something?" I asked Brooke, unsure of what she wanted.

She hadn't spoken a word to me in a long time. Just because she was standing there didn't mean that she wanted to talk to me. I didn't want to have the wrong idea and be **embarrassed**.

"You mean, you don't mind talking to me?" Brooke asked me.

I looked at Chanté and said, "I'm going to talk to her real quick, okay?"

Chanté pulled my arm and whispered, "She's been looking at you all week since you've been hanging with me. I knew it wouldn't take long before she wanted to be your friend again. I just wanna know now. Were you using me to make her jealous?"

Was she serious? I started laughing really hard. That was crazy. Where did she get that from?

"Chanté, no way. Why would I want to do something like that?"

She shrugged her shoulders as if to say she didn't know.

"Well, I would never do that. And I don't even know what she wants to talk about."

"Okay. Well, I'll be over there jumping rope."

As soon as Chanté walked away, I said, "Hey, Brooke. What's up?"

"Hey. I know it feels weird with me speaking to you because I haven't said anything in a long time, but I miss you, Morgan."

Just like a person is supposed to tell the truth because their hand is on the Bible, I had to be honest with her. "How could you miss me? I didn't go anywhere. You told me to leave you alone and that hurt my feelings."

"I guess I wanted to pay you back from when you were mean to me on the first day. But I still wanted to be your friend anyway. I guess I just wanted you to understand me. And for you to say that you were hurt by the way I treated you lets me know you cared."

"Yes, I cared. I'm not gonna tell a fib and say I didn't cry some nights because you and Trey weren't my friends anymore."

"I must be crazy to want to be your friend again when you've got a new one, right? I've been talking to Miss Nelson about it. I've been scared that you wouldn't talk to me and let me say that I'm sorry. But she told me to try because you were a nice person, so I guess I'm trying. Can we be friends again?"

"Yes, Brooke. But I need a real **explanation**. You said a long time ago that it was because the other teachers kept saying how smart I was. Is that true?"

"Well, I thought they were going to skip you to the third grade right away. And I didn't wanna be friends with someone in a higher grade than me. Now I know they're only pulling you out sometimes to take advanced classes. Besides that, I liked the way you wanted to help Chanté. That was really cool of you, Morgan. You're a really nice person, and I know that I messed up. Sometimes I can't even eat my lunch when I think about all the bad things I've been doing to you."

I was shocked that Brooke was saying all this stuff. I just wanted her to come to me and say that she was sorry. Day after day, I would look at her, and she wouldn't say anything. I had given up hope. Before Chanté became my friend, God was my good friend. How did I know she was being honest and she wouldn't come back tomorrow acting mean again?

"Yeah. My mom and I decided that I wasn't ready to move to the third grade." Before I said anything else about being her friend, I told Brooke, "One second."

Then I walked a few steps away and prayed. *Lord, every day since my dad left You've been there for me. I don't even need to ask what You would do because this is just what we learned in Sunday school last week. We have to forgive other people as You forgive us. Help me to trust her again.*

I walked back over to Brooke and she was looking down at her feet. "So?" she asked.

"Of course we can be friends, girl!" We hugged real tight.

"But there's one condition."

"And, what's that? Anything," Brooke said.

I yelled, "Hey, Chanté, come here." She ran right over. "It's that all three of us have to be friends."

I guess they both were cool with it because for the last ten minutes of recess, the three of us got along wonderfully. And wonderfully was an adverb.

● ● ● ● ●

It was Thanksgiving Day and the house smelled like home, sweet home. I know it was because Mama was in the kitchen fixing all of our favorite foods. My mom was cooking too, but she made sure she stayed out of Mama's way.

Not only was little Jayden growing and fun to play with, but Mom and I had decorated my room with my favorite color—pink. I was so happy! She had bought new pillows, sheets, and blankets. And everything matched. She also promised that we could paint the walls really soon.

For most of the day, I enjoyed being a hostess. Papa and I were greeting our family and Daddy Derek's family. The cousins that I had been hanging out with came over.

Drake was looking really sad, so I walked over and sat next to him.

"What's wrong?" I asked.

He rolled his eyes at me and said, "I just didn't wanna come, okay? And I don't wanna talk about it."

"I'm just trying to be nice. You don't have to snap at me."

"Leave me alone. You don't understand anyway," he said as he got up and walked off.

*What would Jesus do?* I thought. He would keep trying to turn a frown into a smile. So I followed Drake and said, "What's wrong? I do care."

"You don't care about me. You have two dads now, so you don't have to care. My uncle was the only dad I had. Now that you and your little brother got him, he doesn't have time to take me fishing or come to my basketball practice. I even got a bad grade, and my mom told him about it. And he hasn't even called yet to yell at me about it. He doesn't care anymore. Now it's the holiday and we have to come to his house. And, for what? He doesn't need us when he got his own family."

Drake was almost growling like a mean bear. Before I could cut in and tell him that wasn't true, he walked away again. I went into the dining room and saw my mom setting up the name cards. She had me sitting between her and Daddy Derek. I didn't think that was the best place for me to sit. So before Mom saw me, I knew I would have to do something quick. I wanted Drake to have my seat.

"Morgan, what are you doing?" Mom asked, being on top of everything as usual.

When I explained to her what was going on with Drake, Daddy Derek overheard me and said, "That is so sweet of you. You care about somebody else more than you care about yourself. That's why I love you, baby girl."

"Well, can you share some of that love with Drake?" I asked him.

"I sure can. You know what, I'm gonna go and tighten that boy up right now about those grades." The three of us laughed.

It actually felt good to see everyone smiling and getting along. My mom was smiling because she had her old and new families together at dinner. Mama was smiling because everyone enjoyed her cooking. My cousins were smiling because their uncle was in tune with them, and they were all having a great time. Pretty much, all of us had something to smile about. Everyone—except me.

Sure, it was Thanksgiving and I had a lot to be grateful for. Mommy and Jayden were okay. Daddy Derek and I were getting along great. I had cool friends at school again. I had a pretty new home. My grades were the bomb. Mommy didn't make me move to the third grade early. I had everything a girl needed. But something was still missing—something didn't feel right.

When I was finished eating, I said in a **somber** voice, "May I be excused?"

"Sure," Mom said.

I went to my bedroom and closed the door to pray. *Lord, I really miss my dad. I know that You're with him, so would You please keep him safe?*

Just then Mom came into my room and said, "Hey, Morgan, I wanna show you this neat toy I got you."

Did she really think a toy was going to cheer me up? I didn't want a new toy or a new Barbie doll or a new book. But because I didn't want to ruin her day, I just said, "Okay, Mommy."

We went into her office and turned on her new computer. I wasn't allowed to go in there and mess with anything. But it was nice to check out all her new things. She pushed a button on the keyboard and my dad popped up on the screen.

"Dad!"

"Hey, Morgan, baby doll. I miss you."

It took a second for me to realize that he was looking right at me. "I miss you too, Daddy," I said.

"I hear you've been learning a lot of things in school. I've been getting your letters, and they've really been keeping me going. I know it's Thanksgiving and we're not together, but you're in my heart. And I know I'm in your heart. Now that your mom has her new computer set up, we can stay in touch and talk more often. Is that okay with you?"

"Yes, Daddy! Of course! All I wanted for Thanksgiving was for me to be able to tell you how much I love you."

"You're so precious and so cute. I could just eat you up, muffin bread."

"Daddy!" I said, wanting him to talk to me like a big girl, not a baby.

"What is it, girl? Thank you so much for keeping me going."

"I pray for you all the time, Daddy."

"I know, baby, and keep those prayers coming. I can feel them. God has me covered over here, and I know He's taking care of you back at home."

"I'm so happy to be talking to you, Daddy."

"I can see that big smile on your beautiful face. We'll be able to see each other soon. But, until then, I want you to remember how much I love you. Remember to watch your manners, and remember to listen to your mom."

"I will, Daddy. I promise."

Then he asked, "Tell me, what's the biggest thing you've learned over the past few months?"

I leaned in close so he could see my face real good. "When I was four years old, you told me that attitudes are **contagious**. You said to make sure mine is worth catching. Well, I never really knew what you meant, but I did remember it. Now I know. These last few months I've learned that when you have a good attitude, you can make the world a better place."

"Oh, Morgan. That is so good. Reading your letters

brought me a lot of joy, but seeing your face has just bright-
ened my day with so much charm."

## Letter to Dad

Dear Dad,

   I just spoke to you in person today. That was
super cool. I wished we could have talked longer so
I could tell you what I learned in school this week. I
guess I'll tell you now. We learned **adverbs**.
Slowly, softly, loudly are examples of some. Once
I got **immune** to people not liking me, they liked
me again. I am happy and showing them **gratitude**
that we are getting along. My friend Brooke was
**embarrassed** to ask me to forgive her for treating
me badly. But, once she gave me an **explanation** I told
her all was forgiven. After all, we all make mistakes
and we all need to be forgiven sometimes. Now at
school I don't have to be in a **somber** mood anymore.
My attitude of being happy is **contagious**, and everyone in my class, including Trey, caught the happy bug.
Love you so much, Dad. You made my Thanksgiving
extra special! I'm most thankful you are safe.

         Your daughter,
         Sweet hearted, Morgan

# Word Search

```
Y  C  R  E  M  B  S  P  E  A  C  D
O  E  O  K  O  R  O  K  S  G  F  O
U  M  X  F  I  M  M  U  N  E  S  Y
M  B  L  P  R  A  B  K  G  A  U  O
A  A  D  B  L  R  E  I  R  U  O  U
T  R  D  O  W  A  R  N  A  T  I  R
T  R  U  W  R  D  N  D  T  H  G  B
E  A  L  O  I  V  L  A  I  O  A  E
R  S  L  Y  T  E  E  N  T  R  T  S
P  S  I  R  E  R  A  E  U  I  N  T
R  E  N  O  R  B  R  S  D  B  O  K
O  D  G  F  Z  S  N  T  E  X  C  N
```

**ADVERBS**

**CONTAGIOUS**

**EMBARRASSED**

**EXPLANATION**

**GRATITUDE**

**IMMUNE**

**SOMBER**

## Words to Know and Learn

1) **ad·verb** (ăd'vûrb) *noun*
The part of speech that describes a verb, adjective, or other adverb

2) **im·mune** (ĭ-myūn') *adjective*
Not affected by a particular infection or situation

3) **grat·i·tude** (grăt'ĭ-tūd', -tyūd') *noun*
A feeling of thankfulness or appreciation

4) **em·bar·rass·ed** (ĕm-băr'əst) *adjective*
Experiencing shame or unease

5) **ex·pla·na·tion** (ĕk'splə-nā'shən) *noun*
The act of making something clear

6) **som·ber** (sŏm'bər) *adjective*
Dark; gloomy; moody

7) **con·ta·gious** (kən-tā'jəs) *adjective*
Able to be spread from person to person

## Morgan Love Series: Book 1

# A+ Attitude

### Stephanie Perry Moore
### Discussion Questions

1. Morgan Love is not happy with her life. Her dad is heading off to the Navy, her mom is remarried and having a baby, and she has to attend a new school. Do you think she should be upset with her changes? What are some things you can do when you aren't happy?

2. Morgan feels bad when she learns that her mom is in the hospital. Do you think Morgan should feel bad for her past attitude? What do you think you need grace for?

3. Brooke tries to befriend Morgan even though Morgan wants to be left alone. Do you believe Brooke was right to continue trying to be buddies with Morgan? How can you get people to change their attitude for the better and be nicer?

4. When Morgan goes out with her friends, she tells them she is upset she has a baby brother. Do you think the responses she gets from her friends are good ones? What would you do if you felt like you were truly unhappy with a big part of your life?

5. When Morgan gets attention for being a good student, her friends get jealous. Is it good to be mad at your friends when they get positive attention? What are ways you can make sure you do not get envious of your friends?

6. At church, Morgan tries to cheer up Drake because he does not want to serve the Lord as an usher. Do you think it was a good thing that Morgan tried to help someone else have a better attitude? Do you feel God expects you to help others?

7. Morgan talks to her mom about her feelings. Do you think she was right to open up and tell her mom her struggles? How can you have a better relationship with your parents/guardian?

## I want to write a letter to:

Dear

# Word Keep Book

**Chapter 1**: stationery, vehicle, sassy, dejected, frustrated, rhyme, horrible

**Chapter 2**: torture, degrees, dilemma, complications, soothing, conversations, adjectives

**Chapter 3**: pretending, negative, distractions, mahogany, identity, experience, everlasting

**Chapter 4**: pronouns, productive, annoying, control, errand, landscape, burdens

**Chapter 5**: scrambled, colic, spiritually, similar, preposition, exceptional, refusing

**Chapter 6**: conductor, headquarters, overseas, figured, perspective, stressing, leader

**Chapter 7**: adverbs, immune, gratitude, embarrassed, explanation, somber, contagious

# 4 Bonus English Grammar Pages

**Nouns**

Nouns are a person, place, or a thing.

> Ex. Morgan read a book in the school.
> Morgan is a noun because it is a **person's** name.
> Book is a noun because it is a **thing**.
> School is a noun because it is a **place**.

**Directions:** Underline the nouns in the sentences below.

1. Morgan is eating a peach. (2 nouns)
2. Trey flew a kite in the park. (3 nouns)
3. The clock was broken. (1 noun)
4. Miss Nelson corrected the test. (2 nouns)
5. Six dogs ran across the sidewalk. (2 nouns)
6. Sadie is reading an exciting book about plants. (3 nouns)
7. Brooke painted a pretty picture. (2 nouns)
8. Kyle played the guitar. (2 nouns)
9. Drake answered the question correctly. (2 nouns)
10. John dribbled the basketball. (2 nouns)

**Adverbs**

An adverb is a word that describes an action verb. An adverb describes how, when, and where an action happens. In this exercise we will work on **how** the action happens.

> Example: Morgan quickly did her homework.
> How did Morgan do her homework? Answer: quickly.

**Directions:** An action verb is described in each sentence. **Circle** the adverb that describes the underlined verb.

1. Trey carefully placed his train on the track.
2. Morgan and Brooke swam lazily in the pool.
3. The class cheerfully sang songs in chorus.
4. Chanté accidentally spilled her milk.
5. Bill grumbled loudly during the test.
6. Drake walked slowly into the church.
7. Morgan usually completes her homework as soon as she gets home.
8. Sadie finally stopped snoring.
9. Drake stamped his feet angrily.
10. Morgan's mother nicely reminded her to clean her room.

**Pronouns**

A pronoun is the word that takes the place of a noun. Some common pronouns include: *he, she, it, we, they, them, us, our, his, her,* and *I.*

**Directions:** Rewrite each sentence. Change the underlined word or words to a pronoun.

1. Morgan helped the whole class with their work.

_____

2. Trey played tag with Brooke and Bill.

_____

3. Miss Nelson cleaned off her board.

_____

4. The <u>dog</u> did not bite anyone.

_____

5. <u>Mama and Papa</u> let me help paint the fence.

_____

**Directions**: **Circle** the pronouns in the sentences below. Some sentences may have more than one pronoun.

6. She went to the store with Morgan.
7. Every Saturday, Trey goes to the park with us.
8. At the grocery store, the cashier gave me change.
9. When the sun comes up, he leaves for work.
10. I enjoyed seeing them on the playground.

**Prepositions**

Prepositions link nouns, pronouns, and phrases together. They are also the leading word In the prepositional phrase. Some common prepositions include: *under, over, in, out, between, up, down, by, onto, to, into,* and *through.*

Example:  After dinner, we went to the movies.
Where did we go? Answer: to the movies.

**Directions:** Underline the prepositional phrase in the sentences below.

1. We are going into the woods.
2. Morgan hid by the tree.
3. Kyle climbed up the hill.
4. Trey tossed the ball under the basket.
5. Drake climbed onto the bike.

6. The store is just beyond the stoplight.
7. Chanté was reading a book in the library.
8. Sam went down the stairs to get her shoes.
9. Sadie jumped over the cat.
10. They are stuck between the floors.

# Chapter 1 Solution

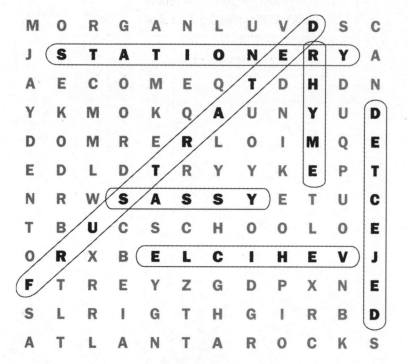

```
M   O   R   G   A   N   L   U   V   D   S   C
J   S   T   A   T   I   O   N   E   R   Y   A
A   E   C   O   M   E   Q   T   D   H   D   N
Y   K   M   O   K   Q   A   U   N   Y   U   D
D   O   M   R   E   R   L   O   I   M   Q   E
E   D   L   D   T   R   Y   Y   K   E   P   T
N   R   W   S   A   S   S   Y   E   T   U   C
T   B   U   C   S   C   H   O   O   L   O   E
O   R   X   B   E   L   C   I   H   E   V   J
F   T   R   E   Y   Z   G   D   P   X   N   E
S   L   R   I   G   T   H   G   I   R   B   D
A   T   L   A   N   T   A   R   O   C   K   S
```

**DEJECTED**

**FRUSTRATED**

**RHYME**

**SASSY**

**STATIONERY**

**VEHICLE**

# Chapter 2 Solution

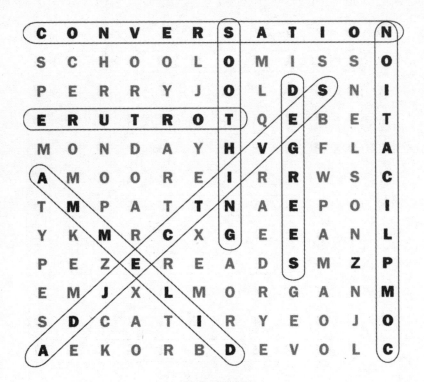

**ADJECTIVES**

**COMPLICATION**

**CONVERSATION**

**DEGREES**

**DILEMMA**

**SOOTHING**

**TORTURE**

# Chapter 3 Solution

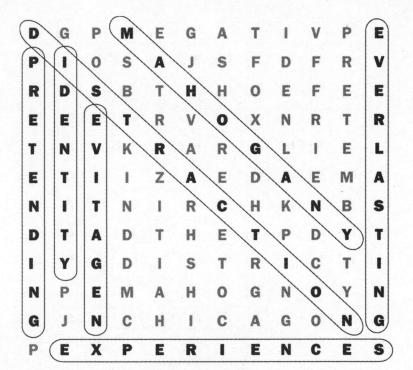

**DISTRACTIONS**

**EVERLASTING**

**EXPERIENCE**

**IDENTITY**

**MAHOGANY**

**NEGATIVE**

**PRETENDING**

# Chapter 4 Solution

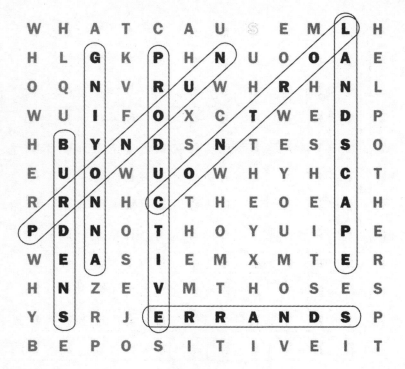

```
W  H  A  T  C  A  U  S  E  M  L  H
H  L  G  K  P  H  N  U  O  O  A  E
O  Q  N  V  R  U  W  H  R  H  N  L
W  U  I  F  O  X  C  T  W  E  D  P
H  B  Y  N  D  S  N  T  E  S  S  O
E  U  O  W  U  O  W  H  Y  H  C  T
R  R  N  H  C  T  H  E  O  E  A  H
P  D  N  O  T  H  O  Y  U  I  P  E
W  E  A  S  I  E  M  X  M  T  E  R
H  N  Z  E  V  M  T  H  O  S  E  S
Y  S  R  J  E  R  R  A  N  D  S  P
B  E  P  O  S  I  T  I  V  E  I  T
```

**ANNOYING**

**BURDENS**

**CONTROL**

**ERRANDS**

**LANDSCAPE**

**PRODUCTIVE**

**PRONOUNS**

# Chapter 5 Solution

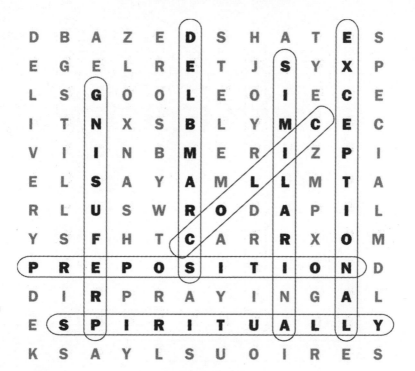

**COLIC**

**EXCEPTIONAL**

**PREPOSITION**

**REFUSING**

**SCRAMBLED**

**SIMILAR**

**SPIRITUALLY**

# Chapter 6 Solution

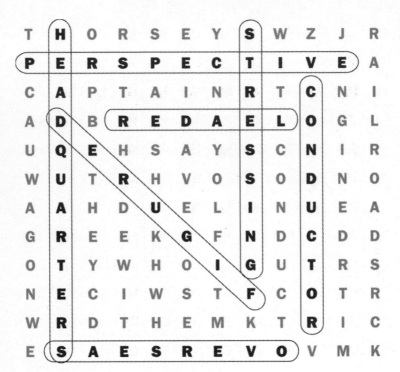

**CONDUCTOR**

**FIGURED**

**HEADQUARTERS**

**LEADER**

**OVERSEAS**

**PERSPECTIVE**

**STRESSING**

# Chapter 7 Solution

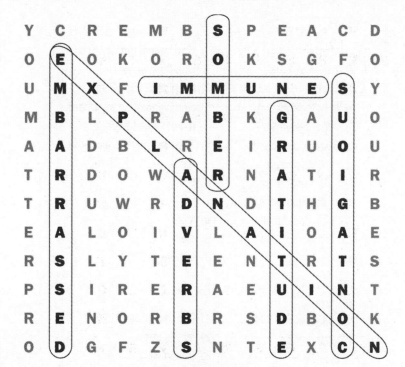

**ADVERBS**

**CONTAGIOUS**

**EMBARRASSED**

**EXPLANATION**

**GRATITUDE**

**IMMUNE**

**SOMBER**

# Answer Keys

## Nouns

1) Morgan, peach
2) Trey, kite, park
3) clock
4) Miss Nelson, test
5) dogs, sidewalk
6) Sadie, book, plants
7) Brooke, picture
8) Kyle, guitar
9) Drake, question
10) John, basketball

## Adverbs

1) carefully
2) lazily
3) cheerfully
4) accidentally
5) loudly
6) slowly
7) usually
8) finally
9) angrily
10) nicely

## Pronouns

1) She helped the whole class with their work.
2) He played tag with them.
3) She cleaned off her board.
4) It did not bite anyone.
5) They let me help paint the fence.
6) She
7) Us
8) Me
9) He
10) I, them

## Prepositions

1) into the woods
2) by the tree
3) up the hill
4) under the basket
5) onto the bike
6) beyond the stoplight
7) in the library
8) down the stairs
9) over the cat
10) between the floors

# Acknowledgments

Recently, I went to the dentist, and though I'm much older than the intended reader, I still act like most kids when it's time to go and get my teeth cleaned. I want to pout. However, this time I prayed before I went, and I decided to have a great attitude about it.

And you know what? I had an awesome visit at Dr. Wolf's office. Everyone was nice. I got my teeth cleaned in the heated massage chair. Although I must confess that I have one cavity, I'm ready to go back.

You see, the Bible says this about man, "For as he thinks within himself, so he is" (Proverbs 23:7). Therefore, if you look at everything from the positive side, then happiness is what you receive.

So be happy, young people. Life may not be perfect,

but know that it can always be worse. God loves you, and that's enough to make anyone smile.

I'm smiling now as I think of all the people who help me write fun books.

To my parents, Dr. Franklin and Shirley Perry, I'm happy because you told me early on that every day is a great day.

To my Lift Every Voice Books team, especially Cynthia Ballenger, I'm so happy to have this opportunity to write books for Jesus Christ with you.

To my precious cousin and assistant, Ciara Roundtree, I'm very happy that you keep working me into your schedule.

To my friends who gave input into this series: Carol Hardy, Lois Barney, Veronica Evans, Sophia Nelson, Laurie Weaver, Taiwanna Brown-Bolds, Lakeba Williams, and Deborah Bradley, I'm happy you care enough for me that you help me to help others.

To my children, Dustyn, Sydni, and Sheldyn, I'm happy that I am able to leave a legacy and that your critiques are part of this project.

To my hubby, Derrick Moore, I'm happy that after sixteen years, we're still pressing on together.

To my new young readers, I'm so happy that you've found this book that I hope will entertain, educate, and inspire you.

And to my Lord, I'm very happy You are not through with my writing career yet and that I have the opportunity to lead young lives to You.